EDWARD KANE AND MR HORSE

COLLECTED SHORT STORIES

VOLUME II

by

Ross Macfarlane KC

ARLAN Press

First Published in the UK in 2025 by

ARLAN PRESS

arlanpress.com
info@arlanpress.com

Paperback ISBN: 978-1-0369-6453-5

Technical assistance in print production by
ScottishPrint, Glasgow (www.scottishprint.com)

Illustrations and cover design by

Lesley-Anne Barnes Macfarlane

In memory of our dear friend,

Neil Beynon, Advocate.

Contents

Introduction

Welcome to the second volume of short stories featuring Edward Kane and Mr Horse.

I say 'short stories', but they turned out a bit longer than usual, so apologies to those of you who are counting the words.

The three Kane/Horse stories in this volume couldn't be more different:

Edward Kane and The Letters of Comfort. One of the great joys of walking in Edinburgh in Scotland is that everywhere you turn, you are reminded of its history. Stroll along Princes Street and stand below the great Scott monument. It's perhaps not well-known that the Scott Monument was designed by a social outsider, George Meikle Kemp – an architect with no formal training, a former joiner's 'mate'! Howls of outrage were heard in the great houses of Scotland's capital when Kemp – the son of a shepherd, no less – won the public competition to design the monument. Added to that, Kemp died in mysterious circumstances before the Monument's completion. It struck me: what would happen if somebody emerged years later and claimed that Kemp was actually a fraud, had stolen the design from another monument – and that person then confessed to murdering Kemp? Read on…

Edward Kane and the Supernal Sisters is based on the explosion of Spiritualism in the mid- to late-1800s. It all started in America, when two wee sisters, Kate and Maggie Fox, claimed that they were getting messages from a dead man through certain spooky knocking and cracking noises in their house. The noises then followed them to other houses. It wasn't long before the girls were giving public demonstrations before paid audiences and answering questions from The Great Beyond on topics as diverse as which stocks to buy to giving advice on 'matters of the heart'. An explosion of other celebrity mediums soon followed, as well as seances taking place in people's homes, and the whole 'craze' (for want of a better word) lasted for the next seventy years.

Regarding the word in the story's title: '*supernal*' - I always loved that word from the old Christmas Carol: '*Unto us a child is born/Sing with choirs supernal…*'. I thought that the word meant '*supernatural*', but when I looked it up, turns out it has a more benign, meaning: '*…heavenly/celestial…of exceptional quality.*' It originated from the old Church Latin word '*supernalis*'– which was the opposite of '*infernal*'!

Edward Kane and The Hanged Man is based on an experience I had when someone insisted on doing a reading of some Tarot cards. I wasn't keen, because that kind of thing always gave me the 'heeby-jeebies' – but the card reader cracked on. Even worse – the reading, in terms of my own situation – proved to be 100% accurate. The whole event proved quite disturbing and, in truth, pretty scary! The more I read about the whole Tarot thing, the more I learned that the cards were not essentially there to predict the future (like, for example the crystal ball) but the readings were meant to be more descriptive of a person's current situation (as it proved to be in my case). I leave it to those interested in that type of *arcana*. But for me…*brrrrr*…

The bonus short story, ***Aunty Fran and Tickler***. I was intrigued by an article I read in the paper that a 90 year-old German gentleman, Heinrich Steinmeyer, a former Waffen SS soldier had left his significant fortune to a tiny Scottish village – Cultybraggen, in Perthshire. Steinmeyer - while still a teenager - had been interned in that wee village during World War II as a German prisoner of war. He recalled that the villagers had all been so kind to him and that some of the local girls had even sneaked him out of the camp and had taken him to the cinema. That - plus the little-known fact that Donaldson's School for the Deaf in Edinburgh was once a Prisoner of War Camp - inspired this wee story of Aunty Fran and her battered violin.

So, once again, please sit back in an easy chair, have a glass of something nice (whether whisky, wine or hot chocolate) and I hope you enjoy the further exploits of our young (impecunious) Advocate and his (irrepressible) Cockney manservant.

'Til next time…

Ross Macfarlane

Parliament House
Edinburgh

December 2025

Edward Kane

and

The Letters of Comfort (2022)

Chapter One

The Changeling

Edinburgh 1852

The Solicitors' Offices of Stevenson and Rose, Writers to the Signet

'The man is clearly an imposter!'

The lady may have been almost ninety, but her proximity to the grave did nothing to temper her white-hot anger. She pointed to the young lady beside her: 'My granddaughter here - my only living flesh and blood - duped! Bamboozled - by a shameless adventurer!' The girl said nothing, but stared at the floor, her cheeks turning a gradual crimson.

Edward Kane, young Scottish Advocate, shook his head: 'Well, Mrs Fordyce, whether Joseph - 'Joe' - Blakemore is an imposter will, at the end of the day, be a matter for the courts to decide. It certainly is an unusual situation…'

'He should be ashamed of himself - thoroughly ashamed!'

The papers that had landed in Kane's work box contained an account of a series of events that were familiar, except for that final twist. Kane looked through his papers:

Two young people get married in a hurry. So far, so ordinary. Soon afterwards, the young man is called to India to serve his country (or in this case - to serve the private army of The East India Company). A common occurrence in the 1840s and 50s. The young soldier is badly injured with others when a nearby arsenal explodes. Unfortunate - but not unknown. After fifteen months' convalescence in a Madras hospital, he is shipped home. A welcome development. Once home to his young bride, the young soldier seems to have changed utterly. So changed, that the young bride's grandmother suspects that the soldier who has returned to them is not the same soldier who left…

'It was the small things that gave him away…'

'Such as?'

The old lady frowned: 'He did not recognise his friends in the street.'

Mr Stevenson, the old solicitor who had instructed the meeting shook his head and spoke in his gentle Aberdonian burr: 'Mrs Fordyce, Mrs Fordyce, it's a sad fact that oor young men are coming back frae war every day, and oftentimes, when they get hame,' Old Stevenson tapped his head with his index finger, 'they are not all there…'

The old lady held up her hand to halt the solicitor's explanation: 'I know what you are going to say, Douglas. But let me put a question to you: am I ever wrong in any important matter?'

It soon became apparent that this was not a lady who was accustomed to be contradicted. The Widow Fordyce continued:

'I'm near blind now. And I'm maybe not as sweet-tempered as I was…' (this struck Kane as something of an understatement) '…but I can still smell a rat. The lad who came back is very cunning. But not cunning enough. He is an imposter. The first Joseph - the one my granddaughter married - against all advice, I might add' - she nodded towards the sobbing girl, 'was a right…a right drinker…'

A sense of embarrassment now filled the room like the vapour of a marshy bog. The young Advocate looked towards the old solicitor. The solicitor, Old Stevenson, puffed on his pipe and nodded: 'Aye, right enough, the lad was often blue bleezin' and staggering aboot the place…'

Kane frowned. Although some of the words were unfamiliar, the sense was obvious enough.

The old lady leaned forward, full of ire, conspiratorial now: 'But the lad who came back… he doesn't touch a drop.'

Edward Kane, Advocate knotted his eyebrows and tried to reason his way through the account: 'But surely, madam, it would have been obvious by just looking at his face…'

It was now the young lady's chance to speak: 'That's the whole thing, Mr Kane, the ammunition blew up in his face, sir. And when he left Scotland, he had a rather bushy beard. But when he came back…'

*****

'…he was clean-shaven.'

Kane sat back in his wing-back chair in his cramped rooms in the Old Town and regaled his Cockney manservant with the events of the day. Mr Horse stroked his stubbly chin: 'So, what are they moaning about, Mr K? The lad goes into the service as a bit of a soak and he and comes back as a goody-two-shoes. Sounds like that young wife got a better deal here.' He grinned: 'And what about in the bedroom, sir, what did she say about that?'

Kane looked coy: 'We did not dwell on the detail, Horse, but I understand that marital relations have not yet resumed.'

'How long was he gone, sir?'

'Five years.'

'Bloomin' eck - if it had been me, I would have had trouble getting me boots off first…'

Kane avoided the somewhat lascivious turn in the conversation: 'Apparently, Mr Horse, the last straw was when the young chap visited a lady who was recently widowed….'

Horse winked: 'I've done that meself…'

Kane shook his head: 'I wager you have Mr Horse. But on this occasion, the chap took the family dog with him.'

The manservant snorted: 'And what's wrong with that?'

The Advocate paused from sipping his tea: 'A dog, Mr Horse. A dog? When visiting a new widow? It's just not done. Let's just say that it's not entirely welcomed in polite society.'

Mr Horse was about to utter an expression not entirely welcomed in polite society - when there was a loud rap at the door. Kane gave a start, then whispered: 'Mr Horse - this month's rent - is it…'

Horse got up from his seat: 'All paid up, Mr K - but I'd know that knock anywhere. That'll be the police, sir…'

'The police???'

But rather than answer his master, the manservant answered the door. Kane heard the door being opened, some cursory conversation in the hallway and then he looked up to see their visitor. Hat in hand, stood Inspector Mackintosh of the Detective: 'Please don't get up, Mr Kane - this is a flying visit.'

Nevertheless, Kane stood up and gave a short bow: 'And to what do we owe the pleasure, Mackintosh?'

The detective stood there, blinking behind his thick glasses. He began to stroke his bushy moustache with the knuckle of his index finger. 'Well, sir, it's…it's…'

Kane smiled, inviting an answer: 'Yes?'

Mackintosh sighed: 'Mr Kane, did you ever hear of 'The Confession Club'?'

*****

Chapter Two

The Confession Club

Inspector Mackintosh sat at Edward Kane's dining table and sipped at his tea from the only good cup in the house. One sip, then the detective widened his eyes: 'I'm bound to say, Mr Horse, I don't think that I've ever tasted tea that is quite this strong. I wager that I could stand a spoon up in it…'

The manservant beamed: 'Thank you, sir. You learn a lot of things in the army.'

Edward Kane smiled. It struck him that the tea was so strong that it could be sold back to the army, cut into chunks and thrown at the enemy causing serious injury. But he said nothing.

Mackintosh of the Detective continued his narrative: 'So, you see, sir, after every major crime, let's say, a great fire or a murder…'
Kane nodded: 'Yes…'

'There is always a…how shall I put it…there is…always…an…an influx of people who report to the Police Office at the side of St Giles. And they confess to committing the foul deed - or whatever it is - that has gained such notoriety.' He sipped at his tea. 'It has become something of a humorism among the police officers at St

Giles that…well, the officers have started calling these individuals 'The Confession Club'.'

The young Advocate nodded: 'Then you have solved those crimes in a remarkably easy fashion, detective.'

Mackintosh grimaced: 'No, Mr Kane. You misunderstand me. The members of 'The Confession Club' - they confess to everything. But they have done nothing. I had a woman last week - must have been in her late seventies - confessed to the recent strangulation of a circus strong-man…'

Horse muttered into his teacup 'Maybe it was his ex-wife…'

Mackintosh continued: '…and so, of course, this string of false confessors, they take up so much police time, but sometimes, just sometimes…'. He sighed and sipped his tea again.

Kane smiled: 'And what is it that vexes you, Mackintosh?'

The detective closed his eyes in resignation: 'We have the confession to a murder. The murder of George Meikle Kemp.'

Silence. Then more silence. Mr Horse shook his head and reached into his waistcoat pocket. He took out a long, clay pipe and a box of matches. Horse took a match out of the box and struck it on the wooden table. The manservant cupped the bowl of the pipe in his left hand and lit the pipe with the match in his right, sending up a series of cloudy puffs as he went. Pipe lit, he shook the match until it was out, then tossed it onto the table. He sat back on his chair:

'Well, gents, I am well and truly bamboozled. Who the heck is George Meikle Kemp?'

Edward Kane looked over at his manservant: "Who WAS, he?', I would suggest. Mr Horse - you are aware of the great Scott Monument in Princes Street?'

'I ain't blind, sir.'

'Well, what you are looking at, Mr Horse, is the vision of George Meikle Kemp…'
*****

It seemed as is George Meikle Kemp had come out of nowhere. And his death was equally mysterious.

In 1836, there was a competition to design a fitting monument for the great Scottish writer, the late Sir Walter Scott. The race soon became bitter. And more bitter still when all of the favourites fell at the fences and the victor was a newcomer with no track record.

George Meikle Kemp – son of a shepherd (of a shepherd, no less!); a man of no real education; a man of no formal training; a so-called 'architect' on the fringes of respectability; didn't he used to be a joiner's assistant?

Surprising, then, that it was his design was chosen after open competition as the winning design for that great public monument. More surprising, perhaps that he did not live to see its completion.

On 6th March 1844, some two years before his magnificent Scott Monument was publicly exhibited to the world, George Meikle Kemp, the lowly-born architect, reputedly the worse for drink, stumbled into the Union Canal in Edinburgh and drowned there. At least, that was the theory.

*****

Mr Horse grinned: 'So, the bloke gets pie-eyed and falls into the canal. We've all done that, ain't we…'

The looks from the other two gentlemen in the room suggested that this was not, in fact, an experience that they had in common with the speaker. He continued: 'Anyhow, this all happened years ago now. How you going to prove the bloke was murdered now?'

Mackintosh put his cup on the saucer: 'Apparently, Mr Lermontov….'

Kane looked up: "Mr Lermontov'?'

'The gentleman who is now – out of the blue – confessing to the murder of Kemp. Apparently, Mr Lermontov kept a diary. And that diary contains conclusive proof that he murdered Kemp. It has names, places and dates…'

Horse bristled: 'But the bloke what confessed to it. He must be off his head, ain't he? Nobody would confess to that. You don't have to waste your time…'

The detective sighed: 'I'm afraid that I do, Mr Horse. There has been the report of a crime. Unusually, it appears to have been reported by the person who committed it….'

Edward Kane shook his head: 'Mackintosh of the Detective, I wager that I could not do your job for all the tea in China.'

'Nor I yours, Mr Kane, because…' the detective began to stumble over his words now, '…because…'. He put his cup and saucer on the table. 'Because, as I understand it, sir, you are about to be instructed. To defend him.'

Kane rested his cup on his saucer. He did not finish his tea.

*****

Chapter Three

A Very Mixed Bag in the Box

Parliament House. The Reading Room of the Faculty of Advocates, where Counsel of all ages and ranks (and the odd judge) mingled (and to this day, mingle), as they chatted and drank coffee together, variously delighted after a famous victory or deflated following an ignominious defeat.

Kane's friend, Collins, Advocate, his horse-hair wig resting on the table, polished his thick horn-rimmed glasses with a small square of silk. He smiled as he spoke: 'Well, my friend, today we are witnessing that rare event in the life of Edward Kane, Advocate. Too much work in the work box! This must be a first for you.'

Kane laughed: 'Collins, my dear friend, no quantity of sows' ears can compensate for the absence of a single silk purse. It's a very mixed bag in that box. On the one hand, a young wife who is not sure if the husband who has returned from India after five years is, in fact, the husband who left and – on the other – a crazed Russian determined to prove that he has murdered Scotland's most illustrious architect.'

Collins got up from his chair: 'Well, my friend remember – a fee is a fee.' He finished his coffee and placed his cup and saucer on the table: 'Just make sure that you are paid in pounds sterling, Edward – and not in roubles…'

*****

'The man was clearly…clearly…an imposter!'

Odd, thought Edward Kane. 'Imposter'. You don't hear a word spoken for years and years and then – twice in the course of a week.

Kane looked at his papers. 'I take it, Mr Lermontov, that you are referring to the late George Meikle Kemp?

'The man I killed. That so-called 'architect', yes.'

Kane looked over at his client. Short, red-faced Mikhail Lermontov, spoke though his thick Russian accent.

The young Advocate had studied the papers, but the lack of a certain answer bothered him. He decided to ask without ceremony: 'So, why now?'

'Why now?'

'George Kemp died in March 1844, sir. It is now December in the Year of Our Lord 1852. You claimed to have murdered him. Why make such a confession some eight years after the event?'

'You know the scoundrel's history?'

'I know that he was a man of humble beginnings and no formal training who bested his betters in open competition – including yourself…'

Lermontov closed his eyes and shook his head. He reached down into a leather bag and produced a large, rolled-up scroll. At first, Kane thought that it was a strip of rolled-up wallpaper, but then the Russian began to make a clearing on the desk and unroll the item. With the aid of some books and ashtrays, he secured the four corners of the scroll, revealing the contents of the entire picture. Lermontov stood back to admire the drawing before him. The faded print, that appeared to be in Dutch, declared: 'Onze-Lieve-Vrouwekathedraal, mrt45'.

The Russian eyed Kane and smirked: 'Clear now, sir?'

'Not in the least, Mr Lermontov. It looks like a set of plans. Plans for the Scott Monument. Therefore – unless I am much mistaken – the work of the late George Meikle Kemp…'

The face of the Russian turned crimson: 'You ARE mistaken, sir, you ARE mistaken…'. He pointed down to the drawing: 'Read it! Read it! This is The Cathedral of Our Lady in Antwerp. Five hundred years old. You see – Kemp – your celebrated George Meikle Kemp, sir – stole the whole design…'

Kane looked up: 'But what is that to you, sir?'

'The world must know the truth. For I am dying…'

*****

Back in the cramped rented rooms of the Old Town, Mr Horse covered his mouth to stifle the laugh: 'So the Russian bloke decides to kill the Scottish bloke because the Scottish bloke has nicked the drawing of a building what belongs to a Belgian bloke? You couldn't make it up, sir. Here's the question: what is it all about, really?'

Kane sat sipping his tea: 'As far as I can gather, Mr Horse, two things: our Russian friend is not long for this world. Apparently, the doctors have given him four months to live and he wishes to clear his conscience.'

Horse gave a low whistle. Kane continued: 'Lermontov says that he went to see Kemp about the theft of the idea, but matters got out of hand – they had a fight and our Mr Lermontov ended up dumping Kemp into the Union Canal. Also, Lermontov feels bitterly the unfairness of the situation. He was one of those who submitted a design for the Scott Monument. His design was rejected in favour of Kemp's winning entry. He wants the world to know that Kemp essentially stole the winning design from an old church in Belgium.'

'I never heard the like, sir. But there's the most important question.'

The Advocate looked up: 'Yes?'

'When are you getting paid, Mr K?'

*****

Chapter Four

Dead Letter

Breakfast time. The cramped apartments of (struggling) Advocate, Edward Kane

'Have you ever killed a man, Mr K?'

'Not recently, Mr Horse…'

The young Advocate's concentration could not be said to be entirely on his manservant, as he was trying to cut off the top of his boiled egg. This was an act of precision with which he was struggling.

The manservant looked up from polishing his master shoes: 'What?'

Kane was pressing down the top of the egg in its cup with one hand and trying to slice it open with a knife in the other. To the objective observer, the words 'heavy' and 'weather' would come to mind. He looked up: 'I'm sorry, Mr Horse, what did you say?'

'I said: 'Have you ever killed a man, sir?''

Kane sighed and shook his head: 'Mr Horse, you have been my manservant these many years. I wager that you have never seen me harm anything. Not even the maggots we found in that leg of lamb that you procured - albeit inexpensively - last week…'

It was the Cockney manservant's turn to apologise: 'Beggars can't be choosers, sir. We done a wery good deal on that leg, though. And once we cut them little blighters out of it....'

Kane put down his knife: 'Mr Horse, I am rapidly losing my appetite here...'

'I've killed men, sir, you know that...'

Kane nodded and nibbled on his buttered toast.

Horse continued: '...at Waterloo, sir...'

The Advocate raised his teacup in salute: 'God bless the Duke of Wellington...'

Mr Horse saluted: 'God bless the Duke, indeed. So, it was one of them French soldiers come at me with a knife...'

This was a tale that Kane knew well. It was an interesting story. The first time around. He looked down at the blunt knife on the table: 'On that subject, Mr Horse, would there be any prospect having these knives sharpened?'

But the manservant was undeterred in his telling of the tale: 'So the French bloke - young, he was, maybe fifteen or sixteen - his name was probably something like 'Shaun France-Waa' - he comes at me and he makes a few passes with his own blade, but he don't see that I've got me little chiv hidden in me hand - the one what I use to whittle wood and the like - and I catches him right under the left armpit...'

'Is there any more tea in the pot, Mr Horse?'

'...and he don't go down straight away, Mr K. He just stands there. He looks like a schoolboy in a uniform what has just been given a difficult sum to do in his head. And then he drops to the ground, like some old blanket what has just been dropped to the floor. So I goes over to the lad...'

'To help him?'

'To go through his pockets sir.'

Kane raised his hands, as if in surrender. Horse scowled: 'Don't look at me like that, Mr K. It was him or me.'

Kane stared at the reluctant egg for a moment, then: 'And what did you find?'

'You mean in the dead Frenchie's pocket?'

'Yes.'

Mr Horse leaned forward in his chair: 'Well, that's the thing, sir. Just a few coins - I think mostly them silver French francs, twos and fives. It weren't a king's ransom, but not to be sniffed at...'

Kane nodded: 'To the victor, the spoils, I suppose.'

'But it was another thing I found, sir.'

The manservant. Looked troubled. This was a part of the story that Horse had never told before. Kane held the silence.

'It was...it was...a letter, sir. I took it out of his pocket. I don't read no French, but at the bottom of if - and I remember this as clear as day - it had the words 'ta mere devouee'. I put it in my pocket, Mr K and it was only later, when I was, you know, getting friendly with one of those Belgian girls what follow the soldiers about - she read it to me and said that it was a letter from the boy's old mum, wasn't it. His old mum. Worried about him. She kept on talking about the glory of France and all, and all I could think of was the lad face down in the mud with the blood stain under his arm. Sometimes, sir, when I get a dose of the morbs, I sit and think of that young lad. Lying there. And his old mum, sitting at home waiting for him…'

Silence for a time, then Kane spoke: 'You did your duty, Mr Horse. You could do no more for queen and country.'

Horse corrected him: 'It was the king, sir. In them days, the king…'

Kane put his cup and saucer back on the table: 'Well, Mr Horse, as enjoyable as this reminiscence is…'

The manservant shook his head: 'Sorry, sir, what I meant to say was this: if your Russian bloke says that he killed the architect fella, and you don't know if he did or not, then ask him what he did straight after. See what that sounds like. Maybe it will ring true, maybe it won't. But ask him anyway…'

At this point, Mr Horse put down the shoe and shoe brush and produced a small knife from his waistcoat pocket. He made his way over to the young Advocate. On reaching the table, the manservant picked up the egg in the eggcup and, with a single, sudden slicing motion, cut the top clean off.

He smiled and held up the blade: 'Same knife, sir. Same knife.'

For reasons upon which Edward Kane did not care to elaborate, the egg remained uneaten.

*****

Chapter Five

Into the Toom

Kane shook his head. 'I'm sorry, Mackintosh - but what are we doing here?'

Sergeant Wilson was meant to be home by this time in the evening, but Mackintosh of the Detective had summoned him to a rickety wooden bridge at Semple Street. The detective looked around them. It was getting dark now, but looking down, he could still see the filthy waters in the canal below. He pointed at the debris in the water: 'His body was found near here, I think.'

Sergeant Wilson sighed, tipped back his stovepipe hat and scratched his mutton-chop side-whiskers: 'Ah, sir - I might have known - the death of George Meikle Kemp. Ye don't let things go easy, do you sir…'

They stood there in the gloaming. Mackintosh shuffled on his feet: 'There may be new information here, sergeant.'

Wilson laughed: 'You mean the wee Russian fella that came in the other day?'

'He claims to have murdered Kemp…'

'What a lot of rubbish, sir. That wee Russian backle…he's so wee, he would need to have climbed a painter's ladder before he could have punched Kemp in the face, sir…'

'Still, we have to follow all leads…'

Their conversation was interrupted by the passing of two youths, both of whom had been rough and rowdy in the approach to the bridge, but were now conspicuously quiet on seeing police officer Sergeant Wilson in his stovepipe helmet and brass-buttoned jacket.

As they passed, Wilson produced a heavy wooden baton from his belt and, without warning, struck one of the boys on the arm.

'Ow!!! What was that for?'

The policeman growled at the lad: 'You KNOW what you did, son. Now get away wi' ye..'

The boys hurried on, one nursing his throbbing arm.

Mackintosh turned to Wilson: 'What did he do, Sergeant?'

The policeman shook his head: 'Nothing yet, sir. But I know his type, he'll do something later….'

Mackintosh stared at the rubbish on the surface of the canal, rising and falling in the gloom. Wilson looked down: 'I was there that night, sir…'

'I know. That's why I called you here, sergeant. To see what you remember.'

The officer scratched his mutton-chop whiskers. 'Ha! What was it? Seven, eight years ago? I had only just got my stripes, like. And I only caught the end of it. Kemp's wife said he hadn't come home. Then we found the walking stick. Then somebody saw a hat bobbing up and doon in the water. Attached to a coat. And that's where they found the body. Down in The Toom…'

Wilson and Mackintosh looked down into the filthy flotsam. 'Where the folk just 'toom' all their rubbish, sir.'

Mackintosh rubbed his chin: 'The question is: how did Scotland's most famous architect end up a as floating body among the stoor?'

'You've seen these crossings after dark, sir. He would have lost his footing…'

'On familiar routes?'

Sergeant Wilson smiled: '
Or he maybe had taken…' he cupped his hand and shook it under his lips, '…a wee bit of a dram, sir.'

Mackintosh shook his head: 'The family say that he was not a drinker.'

'Aye - well the family say more than their prayers, Mackintosh. George Meikle Kemp was a drinker alright. It's just that he only drank the good stuff. I mind that we used to attend at the building site at the monument and he'd be there wi' his cronies moaning that they had run out of the Glenlivet.'

The detective stood, considering this. Wilson continued:

'Of course, if you walk these parts at night, inspector, you''ll always meet bad lads - like that boy I just skelped.' He waved his baton in the direction of the departed youths: 'These lads are aye hanging aboot here looking for mischief. They maybe set aboot Kemp, took his money, then lifted him up and toomed him o'er the fence into the canal. Is that no' maybe it? But for my money, sir, he just had too much of a dram and he took a wrong turn. I remember that night. The fog, sir. So thick, I could hardly see my hand in front of my face.'

Mackintosh stood in silence. Sergeant Wilson put the baton back in his belt: 'I know what you're thinking, sir: could that wee Russian fella have took on Kemp in a fair fight?' He stated to walk away: 'If I was you, I'd get out your Russian dictionary and ask him direct: 'Do you own a pair of stilts?'.'

*****

Chapter Six

No Smoke Without Fire

Hello?

Mr Horse's voice echoed in that large entrance hall, but the place appeared deserted.

'Anybody here?'

A head appeared through the open door: 'Who's that?'

'It's me, Frank - I'm looking to get some knives sharpened…'

'Sorry about that. I was having a wee kip. These fire-station beds - talk about lumpy…'

The Fire-Station at 188 High Street, Edinburgh served a number of functions. Not only was it the location where the volunteers would assemble every Wednesday to perform their drills, it would also serve as an informal guest-house for those providing services to the Brigade. Thus it was that Frank Stone and his portable contraption were often given bed and board in exchange for his speciality - the sharpening of scissors and knives.

Horse was carrying a canvas sack on his back. He swung it around and let it clatter onto the stone floor. Frank Stone rubbed his hands together as if keeping them warm: 'What have you got for me there, buddy?'

Horse pulled open the top of the bag and pointed inside: 'Scissors, razor blazes and knives, knives and more knives, me old mate..'

Stone whistled: 'Goad-blissus, Horse -a' they knives - are ye opening up a butcher's shop?' He began to take the knives out one by one and examine them. He placed them into two separate piles.

Horse looked around the deserted fire station: 'And where's that dog of yours then? He still going strong? I got a little present for him.'

Stone looked up from his sorting and whistled: 'Scraps! Here boy! Come on, boy - Scrappy, wake up ye wee foozler!'

The sound of a dog's nails scratching on the floor in the other room, then through the door, the emergence of a little fox terrier. Not young, but still nimble and inquisitive. 'Scraps' tapped into the room, head cocked, as if to say 'Why did you wake me up?', his paws resembling two furry snowballs.

Horse crouched down and started a rough tousling of the dog's brown, folded-down ears: 'WHO's a good boy, then…'

Stone nodded over: 'He's crabbit wi' most other folk, but he likes you, Horse, because you aye bring him something.'

Horse spoke to the dog, as if lecturing a young child: 'And today, my furry friend, is no different. Yer old mate, the Horse, has brought you…' with a flourish, he produced a piece of crumpled newspaper from his coat pocket: '…this!' Inside the paper were various scraps of meat. The fox terrier tucked in. Horse laughed: 'I knew I was coming here, so I put aside some bits and bobs for our little friend here.'

Frank Stone was still kneeling, examining the knives and putting them into separate piles: 'You never thought of getting a dog, buddy? They like you.'

Horse shook his head: 'Dog? Got enough on my plate looking after an Advocate.'

'And how's that going?'

The conversation turned to Horse's life as a manservant. He made his friend laugh with some (almost true) tales. Stone stood up: 'Right - I'll get the machine going…'

With that, he reached over and took the dog by the collar and led it over to what looked like a large hollowed-out drum suspended off the ground and standing on its side. He lifted up the animal and placed it inside the drum and the dog began to walk slowly. The drum began to turn. Horse watched as a long pulley from the drum began to pull and turn the sharpening lathe.

'Scraps - move it, boy!' The dog, who at this point appeared to exhibit a good grasp of the English language, began to move faster. And as the dog moved faster, the drum moved faster. As the drum moved faster, the great wheel of the lathe began to spin around.

Frank Stone held one of the knives against the spinning lathe and sparks began to fly. He shouted down to the dog. 'Good boy!' Stone picked up knife after knife and held it, sparking against the spinning wheel. And as he sharpened, he spoke: 'So what's your Advocate working on just now, Horse?'

Horse was now sat on a stool, smoking a long clay pipe: 'Two things. First, there's a bloke what says he killed George Kemp…'

'What - Kemp the monument man?'

Horse nodded: 'The same.'

'Well, good luck with that. It was the drink that killed Kemp. Blind drunk and fell into the canal. Everybody knows that. What else?'

'Well, there's a bloke - he went out with the East India Company. So, he comes back and the wife says it weren't him that come back at all, it's another bloke pretending to be him, like.'

'How long was he away for?'

'Five years, I think it was.'

Silence for a time, while the knife-grinder examined his handiwork, holding up and scrutinising the newly-sharpened blades. Then he spoke: 'It changes a man, though, Horse. You know that. I've been away - you've been away - and we've come back and - after everything you've seen over there - everything looks different.' He wiped a rag across the blade: 'Where was he posted?'

'Madras'

Stone laughed: 'Haha - me an' all. Seven years I was there.' He nodded down to the lathe. 'That's where I saved the money to buy this contraption.'

Horse thought for a moment, took a long draw from his clay pipe, then: 'The lad what came back goes by the name of Joseph Blakemore…'

The knife-grinder began to laugh again: 'I knew Joe Blakemore. Knew him well. I was there the day the munitions blew up in his face and him and the other boys got took to the surgeons. I used to bring him his letters in hospital. Oh, that was a hellish place.'

No words were spoken as the dog kept the drum moving and as the pulleys on the drum kept the lathe spinning. Frank Stone pressed the blade against the lathe, frowning in concentration as the orange sparks flew from the blades.

Horse considered this for a moment, then: 'And if I was to take you to see this Joseph Blakemore, Frank, do you think you'd know him now?'

*****

Chapter Seven

Good for the Soul

The Police Office at the side of St Giles Cathedral.

'And you know precisely why you are here, sir?'

'Da.'

'I would appreciate it if you would speak English, since we are, after all, in Edinburgh.'

''Yes', then.'

There was a palpable feeling of tension in the interview room as the parties sat there carrying out their duties. Mackintosh of the Detective, notebook open before him on the table, Edward Kane, Advocate, then the confessor's solicitor, Richard Barrowman – a tall, thin and nervous man - and, at the centre of the interview, Mikhail Lermontov - self-professed murderer.

The detective leaned forward and studied the figure before him. Across the table, self-declared suspect, Lermontov, had a little flaming red face that seemed to glow in the gloom. Mackintosh had the fleeting vision of a podgy marshmallow being toasted. The detective continued: 'Then you will appreciate that you are being interviewed under caution.'

The Russian tilted his head back and rolled his eyes: 'I came to you - not you to me.'

'And you claim to have killed George Meikle Kemp.'

The Russian nodded: 'Da…yes.'

Mackintosh licked the end of his stubby pencil and placed the lead point onto his little notebook: 'Would you care to tell us what happened, sir?'

Lermontov folded his hands: 'I had never met your so-called 'architect', Kemp socially, you understand. He was a peasant, after all. Kemp was of low birth and I am what you, in your country, might call a 'noble-man'. It was, oh, eight years ago. I was in Scotland to search…my…my…'ancestor-hood'…I think it is called'

Barrowman, his solicitor, intervened and addressed the room: 'He means 'ancestry', gentlemen.'

The Russian nodded and repeated the word: 'Da…my family ann-sess-tree…'

The detective looked over: 'Your ancestry, sir?'

Barrowman interrupted again: 'The Lermontovs are originally from Scotland, inspector. When the 'Learmont' family moved to Russia, they were assimilated as 'Lermontovs'.

'Da…yes, is true.'

Mackintosh shook his head and sighed: 'My goodness. Every day is a school day. Please continue.'

'Your Walter Scott - a writer of genius…'

The detective looked up: 'You have read our Walter Scott, sir?'

The Russian nodded: 'Da - but in French, of course…'

Mackintosh sighed: 'Of course. And what of Kemp?'

Lermontov scowled: 'I had heard of your great 'architect' - George Meikle Kemp - and he appears…he appears out of nowhere. And then I saw the plans. The plans for your….how you say…ah - 'celebrated' design for the monument. Clearly…an insult and an act of theft.'

'In what sense, sir?'

The Russian sighed: 'Why do I tell my story again and again…'

It struck Edward Kane at this point that this might prove to be a long consultation. His mind began to wander. Even if he were to be paid in roubles, then how many roubles to the pound? But the mention of his own name brought him back to the surface.

'My….how you say… 'attorney'…'

''Advocate', Mr Lermontov…' corrected his solicitor.

'My Advocate, Mr Kane here - he has seen evidence…'

Kane now felt all eyes on him. He spoke up: 'I…um…Mr Lermontov has furnished us with some designs.' He turned to his instructing solicitor: 'I think that Mr Barrowman has….'

Barrowman, solicitor, anticipating this part of the consultation, had already taken the plans for Antwerp Cathedral out of his case and he now began spreading them over the table. Once secured and visible, the Russian considered the drawings, gave a sneer and swept his hand over the document: 'Need I say more, gentlemen? 'The case', as you would say, 'is closed', is it not? Need I say more?'

Mackintosh squinted at the drawing. He moved his lips as he noted down the unfamiliar writing on the scroll: 'You'll need more than this, Mr Lermontov. You claim that you took the life of another man and your evidence appears to consist entirely of this drawing of an old church.'

The Russian flared up: "An old church?' Do you not see, sir, that this is an exact copy of the design that Kemp claimed to be his own? The man was a thief.'

The detective pointed down at the plans: 'I don't see the relevance of this, sir. Whether Kemp stole it or not - that was a matter for the judges of the competition, was it not?'

The Russian was almost shouting now: 'But I tell you, I am guilty of a crime, sir'

Mackintosh groaned and stopped writing: 'I agree, sir. Wasting police time. That's a crime. I think that we have heard enough.'

Lermontov was insistent. He grabbed the document from the table and began to roll it up again. 'I took this map - this very map in my hand - and I struck him on the face with it. As my ann-sess-tree would strike a man in the face with a glove give challenge to a duel. I cried: 'You are a thief, sir - a peasant and a thief'.'

Mackintosh began writing again: 'And what did Kemp say?'

'Nothing! He said nothing. Proof of his guilt. No answer to the truth.'

The detective sat back in his chair, puffed up his cheeks then blew out the air. He sighed and leaned forward: 'And what happened then?'

A wild look in Lermontov's eyes now, as his grasp of English started to fragment: 'Then, sir, then Kemp stood back and...he start to get...start to get...what's is the word...' The Russian was rapidly clenching and unclenching his fingers as if to catch an invisible fly. '...he start to get 'un-dressed'...'

*****

Chapter Eight

A Sharp Lookout

Stone stood there, arms folded. 'Now, look Mr Horse – I cannae be waiting aboot here a' day. I've got tae get back tae my work…'

Manservant, Mr Horse and knife grinder, Frank Stone had been standing at the corner of Darnaway Street and Wemyss Place for some forty minutes now. Attempting to remain inconspicuous had proved difficult, giving the little barking fox terrier at Stone's feet.

Horse looked down the street: 'He will come, Frank, he' will come…'

'Aye -and so will Christmas…'

Having called at the door of the home of the returning husband (and alleged imposter), Joseph Blakemore, Horse had been informed by the housemaid that the master had gone for his evening walk, but was expected back in around 30 minutes. Would he like to leave a message? No, thank you.

Thus it was that Horse and Stone (and the dog) waited nearby for Blakemore's return. A curious trio on the corner, Horse had attempted to lighten the scene by giving any passer-by a cheery 'Good evening'. While this was reciprocated by a number of smiling nursemaids passing while pushing perambulators, it did not seem entirely welcomed by others – who conspicuously increased the speed of their steps.

Horse pointed towards Stone: 'Now, Frankie boy, you're sure you'd recognise him?'

'I telt ye – I kent him well before that ammunition blew up in his face. He had a big black beard and they had to shave if off so they could treat him. And then, of course, his heid was covered in bandages…'

Horse shook his head, doubtful: 'But there must be other things. Like things that you done together.'

Frank Stone stood frowning in thought. Horse continued: 'You must have got up to some scrapes over there. Just the two of you. Things that only you and Blakemore would know about.'

Stone nodded: 'Right enough…there was that time…when…'

Horse, desperate for information, stared at the knife grinder: 'Yes…'that time when'…?'

'That time when…when…when we ate a monkey.'

This reminiscence stopped Horse in his tracks. It was not the conversation that would be expected in the New Town of Edinburgh. Horse frowned and was silent for a time. Then felt compelled to ask: 'The monkey. What did it taste like?'

'Put it this way, it was better than the rat…'

The unusual culinary reverie was interrupted by the approach of a gentleman turning the corner. The man fit the general description of their quarry. Horse dunted Stone with his elbow: 'What about him? Is that him?'

Stone peered over: 'It could be…'

Horse shoved his friend in the direction of the approaching figure: 'Go on, my son…'

Frank Stone strolled toward the approaching man. The two passed each other. Stone smiled. The man gave a perfunctory bow and went on his way. Then Stone stopped and looked back: 'Joe? Joe Blakemore?'

Joseph Blakemore turned around and scrutinised the figure before him: 'Can I help you sir?'

The knife-grinder walked up to him: 'Do you not know me, Joe?'

*****

Things were getting more and more heated in the tiny interview room in the police office.

Mackintosh of the Detective read from his notes: 'So, Mr Lermontov, you confronted George Kemp, you struck him on the face with that…'

The Russian nodded. He held up the folded scroll and gave a sudden swat down onto the desk, making others at the table start. He smiled: 'I strike him in the face with the very church he has stolen.' He examined the rolled-up document somewhat theatrically: 'Maybe there is still a mark of Kemp the thief on it…'

Mackintosh pressed on: 'And at that point, you say, he began to get….'undressed'???'

The Russian stood up and mimicked the actions he was describing: 'First, he put down his stick-for-walking. Then he took off his hat and put it on ground. Then, he took off the coat and put it on ground – but he folds it – gentle – first….'

Lermontov's solicitor interjected: 'I think that we all know, sirs, that Mr Kemp was reputed to be a very…'particular' gentleman.'

The would-be murderer continued: '…then the Kemp puts up his arms like this.' Lermontov raised his arms and clenched his fists into a boxer's pose. 'So, I picked up his stick and I strike him on face…'

'His own walking cane?'

'Da…yes…'

Mackintosh frowned: 'You challenge him to a fight, and then you use his own walking stick as a weapon against him? It hardly seems fair or…'gentlemanly', sir…'

'Kemp is no 'gentleman', sir. I am. Those rules do not count for him. Also, he is bigger than I am…'

Silence in the room for a moment. Then the detective placed his pencil on his notebook: 'And?'

'I put the stick in his face. He falls back. I look to the sky. I see the full moon. I have the strength of a man who is mad or an animal. Water below. I grab Kemp by collar and drag him to little wall. I lift him over. Splash.' He brushed his hands together as if clearing dust from them. 'The thief is dead.'

Mackintosh looked up: 'And where did all this happen?'

Lermontov's solicitor piped up: 'My client is not from these parts, but I understand that the confrontation is likely to have taken place near Fountainbridge…'

The Russian shook his head: 'Nyet…nyet…no. I saw no fountain. I saw only bridge. Over the bridge. The body falls over the wall into water. Goodbye, thief.'

The silence in the room was disturbed only by the scratching Mackintosh's pencil on his little notepad. He stopped writing and looked up: 'I think we've heard enough, sir.' He looked around the room: 'Does anybody have any questions?'

No-one said anything. The detective leaned back in his chair, frowning. He sat reading through his notebook. Then he became aware of someone holding up their index finger. Edward Kane, Advocate looked like a schoolboy trying to catch the teacher's attention.

'Yes, Mr Kane?'

Kane turned to his client: 'Mr Lermontov. I perhaps ought to have asked you this before, but after the confrontation that you have described, the argument, the, um, fisticuffs,' he raised his fists to illustrate, 'and your depositing Mr Kemp into the Union Canal…'

'Da?'

In actuality, Kane had no question, but he remembered Mr Horse's story of the encounter with the young French soldier.

'My question is: what did you do immediately afterwards?'

The Russian narrowed his eyes.

*****

Chapter Nine

A Dog's Hind Leg?

The knife grinder frowned: 'Do you not know me, Joe? Do you not know yer old buddy?'

Having lain in wait for their victim for almost an hour, manservant Mr Horse, knife grinder, Frank Stone and dog, Scraps, now had him firmly in their sights. Frank Stone had pretended to pass him by, but had then greeted him.

The question now was whether Joe Blakemore (if indeed it was the real Joe Blakemore who had returned) would recognise an old drinking buddy from his time in Madras. So far, the signs were not promising.

The accosted Blakemore studied the knife grinder's face: 'You'll excuse me, sir. My memory is not what it was. I had an accident when I was overseas…'

Stone nodded: 'I ken, buddy – I was there when it happened.'

Blakemore smiled: 'Of course…of course…Frank…Frank Stone…'

The knife grinder smiled: 'The one and only. How's it hanging with you, buddy? And how's that wee bit of jam you were married to?'

'She is…she is…'

'Women problems, eh? Same old Joe.'
He frowned: 'No…I think I'm different now…'

At this point, the little fox terrier padded up and licked Blakemore's hand. He withdrew it with a start. Stone laughed: 'Don't mind my wee Scraps there. He disnae bite. I'm surprised he's taken to you. He disnae really like folk.'

Blakemore knelt down and stroked the dog's head. 'Maybe he just doesn't trust people.'

'Never remember you being a dog lover, Joe.'

'Well – people change, Frank.'

Stone introduced his old friend Joe Blakemore to his new friend, Mr Horse – 'Wery pleased to make your acquaintance, sir.' – and the conversation turned to general reminiscence. After a time, Blakemore took out his watch from his waistcoat pocket: 'My word, is that the time?'

Stone, sensing that this might be an overture to an attempted departure, cut in: 'Right, Joe – me and Horse are just on our way to one of thae wee snugs in the Old Town – and you are coming with us, boy.'

Blakemore raised his hand in resistance, but the knife grinder's tone took on a certain sharpness now: 'What's the matter wi' you, Joe? You think because you've got a top hat on now, you're too good to have a wee dram wi us?'

The top-hatted figure stood genuinely conflicted. Stone could sense the old friend softening: 'Come on, buddy. Like we used to sing thae News Years when we were thegither in Tamil Nadu – 'We'll tak' a cup of kindness yet – for auld lang syne….''

A pause. Then a nod of resigned agreement. Then, four figures – a knife-grinder, a manservant, a potential fraudster and a dog – made their way towards the Old Town.

*****

'I do not understand the question, sir.'

Edward Kane leaned forward: 'it's not a trick, Mr Lermontov. All I am asking is: after you had dumped the body of George Meikle Kemp into the river, what did you do immediately afterwards?'

The Russian thought for a moment, then: 'I remember clearly. I could see his body floating on the water. And the hat. And the coat. And I looked up to the sky. The clear, blue starry sky. And the moon. The full moon. Smiling down on me. Smiling because justice had been done.'

Kane noted this down. This nocturnal observation hadn't appeared in the Russian's previous account (but why should it?). Mr Barrowman, Lermontov's solicitor took a black notebook out of his case and placed it on the table. 'Gentlemen, this is Mr Lermontov's personal notebook. An occasional diary of sorts. He informs me that the relevant information – date and time etc. – is contained within. Although, I should inform you that it is entirely in his native language of Russian.'

Mackintosh lifted up the notebook and examined the contents. Some of the lines were short, like poetry. 'You understand that it will take us a few days to have this looked at, sir.'

The solicitor smiled: 'Of course, he understands that. Our client is satisfied that you will find the contents satisfactory. He will present himself for arrest at your office this coming Friday and you may charge him then. He will put his affairs in order in the meantime. Until then, I have arranged a set of rooms for him at The New Club and you may find him there. Any more questions?'

*****

'Come on Joe – rack those brains, boy! The name of that doctor. You mind – in the hospital – the fat one…'

Joseph Blakemore may or may not have realised it, but he was being mined for information to confirm (or otherwise) that he was the real McCoy. He paused for a moment, then: 'Yes. The big fellow. Dr Wiggins…'

'And we used to call him?'

'Of course – 'Piggy Wiggins'. How could I forget…'

The pub was noisy and the rum was strong. Mt Horse – no stranger to intake of hard liquor – watched carefully as his friend, Frank Stone gulped down his fourth glass, while their gang-pressed friend was still sipping at his first.

Stone pointed to the glass: 'And look at ye – you're a proper gentleman now – but you're drinking like a lady. Get that down ye!'

Blakemore shook his head again: 'Honestly, I must be going…'

Stone adopted an offended tone: 'But I've not finished my story yet. I was just telling my pal, Horse, here aboot our time in Madras. Ye remember thone time when we ate that thing we said we'd never eat? And we said we'd tell nobody. Remember, buddy?'

Blakemore gave a rueful smile and shook his head. Stone had already told Mr Horse that he and his friend, while in Madras, had feasted on monkey flesh. They had kept that fact to themselves. Surely this bizarre dish was something that Blakemore could not have forgotten. The knife-grinder insisted: 'Ye mind, Joe, ye mind? It was the same time – the camp had ran out of food – and we shot and ate thone rats…'

Blakemore, who was sipping his rum, put down his glass and raised the index finger of his right hand: 'Yes – of course – the rats. Disgusting…'

Stone frowned: 'You said they were delicious…'

His friend started to get up: 'Well, needs must. Now, I really ought to…'

Frank Stone placed a hard hand on his shoulder and pushed him back down onto his seat. Not gently. 'You're going nowhere, buddy. My friend here thinks that you're a fake. So, come on – what was that thing that you and me ate and we swore we'd never tell anybody?'

Blakemore sighed and stared at the floor.

*****

Chapter Ten

Four Months to Live

Lermontov had already left the room and had slammed the door. Mackintosh, solicitor Barrowman and Kane sat in an embarrassed silence for a while, before the detective spoke to the solicitor: 'How long does your client have to live?'

'Well, he says that the physicians gave him four months. But you know what they're like, detective. The doctors give you four months and it looks good when you live for twelve.'

The quip broke the ice and all laughed.

The solicitor continued: 'And he is certainly making the most of his remaining time here. He appears to sleep little.'

Mackintosh nodded: 'He clearly comes from money.'

Barrowman reached down into his briefcase and produced an envelope: 'A Letter of Comfort authorised by the Bank of England.' He reached down again and produced a cloth bag: 'And – forgive the theatricality, but this is what he did at our first consultation.' He proceeded to dump the contents of the bag onto the table. Out flew dozens of notes that looked like foreign currency. Each person at the table picked up a note and examined it. The solicitor continued: 'Mr Lermontov has suitcases full of these'

Mackintosh of the detective felt the note between his fingers: 'Suitcases full of bank notes?'

The solicitor smiled: 'More precisely, these are 'State Credit Notes'. Perfectly legal tender in Russia. I have seen them before, but never in such quantities.'

Edward Kane pointed to the collection of notes on the table: 'But I don't see any numbers, any....'

The solicitor picked it up: 'No denominations, you are correct, Mr Kane. In my experience of this type of currency, the value of each note is written in words – unfortunately, in this case, in Russian.'

Mackintosh placed the note back onto the pile and leaned back in his chair: 'Well, I don't know what you gentlemen think about this whole thing, but I'm flummoxed. How much money did Lermontov bring over with him?'

Barrowman began to scoop the notes back into the bag: 'By all accounts, several thousand pounds. We took the suitcases to the new Commercial Bank in George Street, but they couldn't deal with the sheer amount of roubles – so we've sent them to The Bank of England in London for exchange. I'm optimistic to hear by the end of the week. And then we will issue Mr Lermontov with a passbook containing the final balance.'

As if reading the young Advocate's mind, the solicitor smiled over to him: 'And then Mr Kane and I will be paid. In pounds sterling.'

*****

Mr Horse and Frank Stone were staring at Joseph Blakemore now. On the face of it, Stone's question was simple: when out there in Madras, what did Stone and Blakemore kill and eat that was such a secret?

The knife grinder, on his fifth rum, was starting to get obstreperous: 'I've got a better idea. What about we just take you to the police office now and tell them that we've proved that you're a fake, eh, 'Joseph' – or whatever your real name is?'

Blakemore was silent for a time, then: 'A tufted grey langur.'

Mr Horse leaned in: "A tufty what?'

Blakemore gulped down some rum: 'A kind of monkey. A tufted grey langur. He was just licking moisture off the leaves. And I shot him. And we skinned him and cooked him and ate him…'

Frank Stone raised his glass: 'And he was bloody delicious an' all. Good work, Joe.'

'…and we never told anyone. He's considered sacred there. To do with the god, Hanuman. We kept it quiet. Didn't want to upset the locals.'

With that, he downed his rum. He got up from his seat and tossed some coins onto the table: 'And now – if you don't mind…'

*****

Two hours later. Same pub. The knife grinder (on his seventh rum): '…and tae think – after his face was near blown aff – I use to visit him every week. In that hospital. I'd sneak him a wee dram. Maybe give him his letters from that lassie at hame. And look at him noo – eh, Horse?' He mimicked the more recent incarnation of his old friend. "And now – if you don't mind'. Well, I DO mind…I DO mind, buddy…'

Horse smiled: 'Francis Stone – I think it is time for you and your faithful mutt to get back to that fire station and hit the hay, my friend.'

Stone was undeterred: 'Every week, Mr Horse – into that stinking hell-hole they called a hospital. You should have seen the place. Never seen so many beds. So many people. They men were packed like sardines in a tin.'

Horse finished his drink. 'Well, chum – at least we solved the mystery tonight. The bloke what came back is definitely Joseph Blakemore.'

Frank Stone laughed: 'Oh, Horse, Horse – buddy, you've no' go a clue, have ye?'

Horse frowned: 'But he knew about the monkey and all…'

'Monkey my eye! I don't know how he knew about that, but that fella isnae Joe Blackmore.'

'How do you know?'

Stone lifted the fox terrier onto his lap: 'The dog. Joe Blakemore hated dogs. In Madras, they're runnin' about the streets, 50tarving'. Joe would just fire guns at them for sport. But ma wee Scraps here,' he nuzzled the dog's head, 'Scraps liked that fella here wi' the top hat and the fella clapped him and everything. That's no' Joe Blakemore.' He scratched the dog's ears: 'People lie all the time, Horse. But dogs don't lie. Dogs don't lie.'

*****

'Mr Horse, you are late.'

The manservant was taking off his coat: 'Sorry, Mr K – lost track of the time. I was out working, sir.'

'You don't smell as if you've been working, Mr Horse.'

'Had to show willing and down a few glasses so that the bloke don't suspect, sir.'

With that, Horse narrated the events of the day to his master. The Advocate knotted his brows: 'So, your friend, the knife grinder, is convinced that this fellow is a fake because the Blakemore who left Scotland did not care for dogs and the Blakemore who returned does. I hardly think that that argument would persuade a judge.'

Mr Horse – not entirely sober, given that he had been out 'working' – grinned: 'We could always put that little fox terrier on the stand, sir' He mimicked swearing the dog in: 'Could you raise your right paw…'

'Mr Horse, I venture that you have been 'working' too hard. Any sign of supper on that hard-working horizon? An early night tonight – we have court tomorrow.'

*****

Chapter Eleven

Clever Dick

The Great Hall at Parliament House was full to the gun-holes today. The Advocates – in what from a distance might have looked like an infestation of black beetles with curly cream heads – were swarming around the highly-polished polished floors, some in pairs, some in obvious dispute with their clients, others in conspiratorial huddle with their law agents.

'Oh, my sainted aunt – what is SHE doing here?' Pointing with his elbow, solicitor, old Mr Stevenson nodded to Edward Kane and then nodded towards the front entrance. Through the crowd, there at the entrance, shaking her umbrella, was The Widow Fordyce, grandmother of the young lady who had questioned the identity of the returning husband.

Kane smiled: 'Well, at least she didn't bring the granddaughter with her.'

And, as if on cue, Esme Blakemore (nee Fordyce) – hereinafter referred to as 'the granddaughter' – appeared at the entrance.

Old Stevenson edged towards the great open fire: 'Perhaps, if we keep out heads down and we are lucky, she will not find us until the hearing is over…'

This was not to be. Kane was soon aware that the old lady was waving over to them. Not so much a greeting, more akin to the waving down of a taxi carriage. She made her way over with her granddaughter following. Stevenson gave a short bow: 'Mrs Fordyce – what a pleasant surprise.' Kane took a bow, but looked at his shoes. The solicitor continued: 'As I have advised you, madam – and I dare say, on more than a single occasion – there is no requirement for you to attend EVERY hearing…'

The Widow Fordyce glowered: 'I am the client. I have a right to be here…'

Stevenson stifled a groan: 'Mrs Fordyce, you are NOT the client. The client is your granddaughter here,'. He turned to the young lady: 'Good morning, Mrs Blakemore…'

Esme Blakemore curtsied and the gentlemen bowed.

The old lady was having none of it: 'Client or not – I am the one paying the bills here with these – what seem to me to be exorbitant – fees. I may be almost blind, but I have a right to see how my money is being spent.'

The lawyers had been out-argued by this basic point and accepted their fate. But Old Stevenson had his parting shot: 'I would remind you, madam, that Mr Kane, your Counsel here, has agreed to conduct your case on a speculative basis and it would be wise to bear that in mind.'

Suitably chastened (for now) the old lady followed her lawyers through the bewigged throng until they came to the wall upon which today's business was posted. Here was a list of cases and (more importantly) a note of the judges who were down to hear those cases. Kane gently manoeuvred his way through the group of Advocates so that he could peek in and read the daily list. On his return to the group, the young Advocate looked noticeably worried.

The solicitor asked: 'And who did we get today, Mr Kane?'

'We appear to have, um, well, you can see for yourself'

Stevenson narrowed his eyes and peered at the listings on the wall. 'Oh…'

It was apparent to the ladies there that the solicitor's 'Oh…' was not a good 'Oh…'.

The Widow Fordyce leaned in: 'Is there a problem, gentlemen?'

The solicitor said nothing for a moment, before muttering – almost to himself – 'Clever Dick…'

*****

If there was a problem with Lord Dick, it was that he considered himself too good for the job. Alexander Mills Dick had risen through the ranks of the Faculty of Advocates with breath-taking speed and had soon become Counsel of first choice in any case. Elevation to the Court of Session bench appeared guaranteed from day one. And then when that happened, it soon became clear that the appointment had been a catastrophic error.

Because, very soon into the job as judge, Alexander Mills Dick realised that he was bored. An appearance before Lord Dick would typically entail a detailed lecture from the bench on the correct way on how the case ought to have been conducted – and this was not it.

Edward Kane forced a smile: 'It is really a matter of no concern, Mrs Fordyce. The judge, he is very…very 'particular', shall we say. But this is only a formal hearing today. I have agreed with the other side what is to happen, and so it shouldn't take long.'

This did not please the grandmother: 'If you have agreed everything with the other side, sir, then why are you here today? Why are we spending my money? Remember – I am the one whose pocket is being picked here..'

Kane said nothing, but studied the throng of Advocates walking up and down Parliament Hall and spotted his opponent: 'I'm afraid that this is the procedure madam. I shall let Mr Stevenson here explain. I see Counsel for the other side over there, so if you will excuse me…' With that, he gave a small bow to the ladies and left a glowering solicitor to deal with the clients.

The young Advocate called over to his opponent: 'Charles…'

*****

Chapter Twelve

'To Put Her Away Privily'

Kane's adversary in the case, Charles Cod, was well-set, well-meaning and well-liked. They began to promenade up and down the long narrow floors of Parliament Hall. Cod chuckled: 'Edward – what is this I hear that you are now representing a Russian millionaire? Something about the Scott Monument?'

Kane laughed: 'I have the pleasure of being instructed by a certain Mikhail Lermontov – a man determined to get himself into trouble.'

'From what I hear, Edward, your Russian friend is out on the town every night doing just that. Your client appears to be out on the town every evening spending money as if there is no tomorrow.'

Edward Kane nodded. He decided not to tell his friend – as far as Mikhail Lermontov was concerned – that in a mere matter of months, there would be no tomorrow: 'He arrived here with a number of suitcases. All of which, as I understand it, were packed with roubles.'

'That must have been jolly heavy! I've seen those Russian coins…'

Kane interjected: 'PAPER roubles…'

His opponent laughed: 'I've seen those too. Money guaranteed by the state! Oh, Edward, you lucky blighter! I hope you're charging double. For the inconvenience.'

'I see no inconvenience.'

'Keep looking, my friend. Keep looking – you'll find something.' They laughed.

In the Faculty of Advocates, fierce opponents are often firm friends and so it was with Edward Kane and Charles Cod. The conversation turned to this and that and finally to the case in hand. Cod gave a sly smile: 'Edward, I wonder if I might test a theory with you.'

'Of course.'

'The substance of your case – and beautifully pled, by the way…'

'Thank you…'

'The substance of your case is that my client, Joseph Blakemore, went out to Madras with the East India Company and he came back – how shall we put it politely – 'a changed man'.'

'Well put, Charles.'

Charles Cod said nothing for a time and stared at the floor in concentration as they walked down the Hall. Kane interrupted his thinking: 'Do I require to proffer a penny for those thoughts, Charles?'

'Edward, you and I have had a great number of clients…' (Cod was being generous here – Kane had only managed a few so far), '…but can I just say that I have seldom met a chap more genuine than Joseph Blakemore.'

Kane responded: 'The issue here is not whether he's 'a genuine chap', Charles – it's whether he is the genuine Joseph Blakemore.'

Cod laughed: 'Bull's-eye, Edward – bull's-eye! But my theory is this – or perhaps it's more instinct – the wife left behind, sorry, I've forgotten her name…'

'Esme Blakemore – nee Fordyce'

'The lovely young Esme Fordyce is not the principal agitator here, is she?'

Kane was silent. Cod continued: 'It's granny, isn't it?' Kane looked up. Charles Cod went on: 'I've seen that woman here at every hearing, at every stage. I saw her this morning. What on earth is she doing here?'

'Granny holds the purse strings. She is not entirely trusting of the process. Apparently, she wants to understand the mechanism of how her pocket is being picked today.'

Cod laughed: 'Well, I have a number of criminal clients who would be only too willing to give her a tutorial.' He looked over to the fireplace: 'Ah – ecce homo – behold the man, Edward – by the fireplace there, one Joseph Blakemore.'

Kane looked over and saw a well-dressed, earnest-looking figure in greatcoat and top hat warming his hands by the fire. He turned to Cod: 'What is he doing here?'

'I plan to consult with him after the motion. Edward – before you go, I'll let you into a secret. Joseph Blakemore there loves your young lady. He seems an awfully tender-hearted husband. He says that he will do anything to spare the young Esme the ordeal and the shame of giving evidence in public on the stand. Speak to your client.' He laughed: 'More importantly – speak to granny. If we were to, for example, sist the case – kick it into the long grass – we can arrange for a judicial separation here. That kind of thing – not opposed – all affidavits – we can work out the details later.'

This unexpected proposition stopped Kane dead in his tracks. Now the other Advocates walking behind them began to walk around them, like the waters of a stream moving around a stone.

'He knows he's changed, Edward. He's not denying that. But he's also a good husband – he loves her so much – he wants only good for her. Obviously, he has come back a different man. And if she can't accept him as he now is, then, rather than disgrace her with this – if I may say, rather sensational – court action…'

Odd – the things that strike one out of the blue. Edward Kane had a sudden flash of his father, a church Minister, on the pulpit on Christmas Day: 'Then Joseph, her husband, being a just man, and not willing to make her a public example, was minded to put her away privily…'

But it was then that Kane realised that his opponent was no longer looking at him. Rather, he was staring through the crowd to the fireplace. Kane looked over. A roaring fire – but Joseph Blakemore was gone now. 'Everything alright, Charles?'

Cod smiled: 'I just thought…I could have sworn…aaaah,' he nodded his head '…makes perfect sense now.'

Edward raised his eyes in expectation, seeking an answer. Cod laughed: 'My client has just gone off with some pretty little dollymop. The mystery of why he would like a quick 'divorce', as it were, is quickly solved. Of course – he has come back and formed a new connexion…'

Their conversation was interrupted by the cry of a small figure bellowing through a window high up on the wall: 'Call the case – Esme Fordyce or Blakemore against Joseph Andrews Blakemore…'

Charles Cod straightened his wig and smiled: 'You've seen who our judge is today?'

Kane nodded: "Clever Dick'.'

'He's not a bad sort, but I always feel that with him, there's always the sensation of Daniel in the Lions' Den.'

Kane had an unkind thought: In that case, Daniel actually survived.

*****

Chapter Thirteen

The Lions' Den

The judge – Alexander Mills Dick, known to all – with absolutely no affection whatsoever - as 'Clever Dick' sat on the bench, drumming his fingers and looking out of the window: 'I've read the papers here. They seem…competent enough.'

Edward Kane bowed: 'Thank you, my lord.'

'But I don't quite understand what you are asking me today, gentlemen.'

Kane was standing. His opponent was sitting beside him, head down. Charles Cod had a look of a cat that was just about to be hit on the face.

The young Advocate continued: 'It's fair to say that there has been a…development, only this morning, my lord, that may have a bearing on the outcome of the case.'

The judge laughed: 'What 'development'? I've read the papers. Husband goes off to India. An arsenal blows up in his face. He comes back 'changed' – whatever that means. And the wife thinks he's a different fella because he sometimes uses the wrong fork and likes to pat the odd dog. What am I meant to make of that?'

'I hope that the evidence, my lord…'

'The evidence?' Clever Dick shook his head. 'The evidence will consist of you getting your client – a pretty young thing, no doubt – to start crying on the stand and squeak 'Pleeeese, sir'. The plan is to flutter her eyelids at the judge to get what she wants. Well, that stratagem won't work, Mr Kane. I should know. I invented it.'

'My lord, I am optimistic that the totality of the evidence…'

The judge cut across him: 'And what is this lady so exercised about?' He lifted up the Summons and waved it at learned Counsel. 'The 'husband' who came back seems a good enough sort. By all accounts, better than the blighter who left for India. It's as if she has sent off a shilling and got back a pound.'

No use fighting with this type of judge. Kane bowed: 'My lord has my submissions.'

Clever Dick shook his head: 'Before you sit down, Mr Kane, how long do you expect the court to wait for the resolution of this 'development', as you would have it?'

'Well, my client was here this morning, my lord…'. He turned round to his solicitor. No client now. No granny, either. On being called into court, Mr Stevenson, the solicitor had confessed to Kane that he had left the ladies to their own devices for a few minutes and had then lost both of them in the crowded Parliament Hall. This seemed like a blessing at the time.

In fact, the sheer numbers of the crowd and the tumult in the great Parliament Hall had led to another situation. Whether a blessing or otherwise remained to be seen. Stevenson had stepped away to speak to a solicitor friend that he had seen in the crowd; after a few minutes, granny Fordyce had gone looking for Stevenson; Esme Blakemore (nee Fordyce) had gone to look for granny. And in that whirligig of confusion, Esme Fordyce now stood by one of the great fires in Parliament Hall and standing there before her was the returned man who bore the name of Joseph Blakemore. Her first instinct was to turn walk away, but there was such a imploring, tender look on Blakemore's face that she found herself unable to do so. He gave a little bow: 'Esme. Esme – I have the answer. I beg you – please just listen to me. Just for five minutes. I promise. Five minutes. No more.'

So it was that Charles Cod did see his client leave with a beautiful young lady. But the young lady in question happened to be the client's wife.

*****

'Before we go on, Esme, I must prepare you for a piece of shocking news.'

To the casual viewer, this seemed an ordinary couple. A young husband and wife sitting in a coffee shop on the Lawn Market, only minutes from the Court of Session. The casual listener, though, would have heard a tale that was anything but ordinary.

'Joseph Blakemore is dead.'

Esme Blakemore bowed her head and nodded, as if confirming the fact to herself. The man continued: 'You do not seem surprised.'

'I felt that I lost Joe before he left for India. After the wedding, he soon tired of me. He was like that. I fear that it was all about 'the chase' for him. And once he had captured me, I think that I bored him. That's why he chose to go out to India. For…new…'adventures', I suppose.'

There was silence between them for a time, then she looked up and studied the face of the man across from her. 'So – what does that make you? What is your real name?'

'Archibald Greene.'

Another silence, then: 'How do you do, Mr Greene.'

He responded: 'How do you do, Mrs Blakemore.'

She gave a brittle little laugh: 'And now that we have been formally introduced, Mr Greene, you can perhaps tell me what happened to my husband.'

*****

Chapter Fourteen

Letters of Comfort

Archibald Greene nodded and began his narrative:

'Your husband Joseph and I were colleagues. When the ammunition exploded, I was there too. Joe caught the brunt of it, but I managed to drag him to safety.'

Esme Blakemore smiled: 'That was very brave of you. Thank you.'

Greene continued his tale: 'And so we were both taken to the infirmary. A hellish place. Crowded. Dirty. Death and disease all round. My bed was placed up against Joe's. He was very ill indeed and I would help him with daily tasks, eating and such. The days were long. And we would talk to pass the time. I learned a lot about him. I wager that there was not a single, un-kept secret…'

'Yes. Joseph loved to talk. Mostly about himself.'

Greene went on: 'We both had handsome beards at the time and these required to be shaved off before the surgeon could assess the damage to our faces. Then he immediately covered our faces in bandages.' He chuckled: 'As a prank, we would sometimes change places and swap beds - as you can see, we're both the same height and build - and then - because our faces were bandaged - we would pretend to be one another.' He chuckled: 'I would mimic Joe's voice and he would mimic mine – everyone was fooled. It was a way of passing those long hours in that hell-hole of a hospital. That, and of course, your letters. I would read them to Joe, and when it came time to respond…'

Esme gave a kindly smile: 'Mr Greene, those letters from India were beautiful, and…' She stopped herself. A sudden realisation. She looked at the floor. 'I assumed they were from Joseph…'

Greene shot her a timid glance: 'We lived for your letters. No - I was the one who lived for your letters. Joseph was…'

Esme nodded. Tears in her eyes now: 'So those lovely letters…they were from you, weren't they?' An involuntary tear began to run down her cheek. 'Joseph was never much of a correspondent. For him, the world was very much…' she motioned towards the window, '…out there. Whereas, I was always happiest sitting in a corner with a book on my lap. Living in my imagination, I suppose. I'm afraid that he saw me as something of a Blue Stocking.'

Archibald Greene leaned forward: 'No, no, Esme - not at all. I remember well the letter with your analysis of Voltaire…'

She gave a sad little chuckle: 'Mr Greene, I think that you have just proved my point.'

Greene gave a shy smile: 'Yes, it was me. I would reply to your letters. Pretending to be him. And I have kept them, you know. All of them…'

'As have I…'

'…and I would read them again and again, imagining your voice. And, even though we had never met, I came to feel that I knew you. And knew you well.'

The new widow blushed: 'What happened to Joseph.'

Greene leaned back again: 'Of course. One evening, we came up with a ruse. Joseph and I swapped beds at lights-out. We were to play a trick on the evening nurse – pretending to be one another and so forth. I must have fallen asleep, because the next thing I knew, there was a crowd doctors and nurses around my bed. Of course, the person in my bed was not me - it was Joseph. But they didn't know that. And I heard them shouting: 'It's Archibald Greene - he's dead."

The widow nodded: 'They assumed that the fellow with the bandaged face in your bed was you…'

'Correct.'

She wrinkled her brow: 'And what did you…I mean what did 'he' die of?'

Greene shook his head: 'No idea. People were dying around us every day. It just became a way of life.'

'And you said nothing?'

'There was so much wailing and gnashing of teeth - it didn't seem polite to interrupt…'

The lady was dumbfounded: 'What an extraordinary story…'

'Not as extraordinary as when I required to attend the funeral of Archibald Greene - my own funeral. I never want to do that again…'

'I fear, Mr Greene, you may have little choice in the matter.'

With that exchange, newly-revealed faux husband Archibald Greene and newly-revealed widow Esme Blakemore (nee Fordyce) suddenly covered their mouths. And they began to giggle. Uncontrollably.

Then, an extraordinary thing happened. The timid Esme Blakemore reached over and gently touched the face of her faux husband. She smiled: 'Those letters. All the time – it was you…'

*****

'Why am I surrounded by incompetents?'

Lord Dick was shouting now. 'It's a simple question, Mr Cod. What is the nature of this 'development'?' Charles Cod, Advocate began to prepare his response, when he saw that Lord Dick was now staring beyond him at the back of the court. 'And who the blue blazes are YOU?'

*****

'What do you mean, sir - 'And that was it'?'

Horse was drawing on his long clay pipe while Kane sat in the wing-back chair, glass in hand.

'As I say, Horse, that was it. Esme Blakemore appeared out of nowhere and told his lordship that the whole thing had been a terrible mistake. That her husband was a good man and I think she said 'a friend' too…'

'A friend', Mr K? Husband and wife? Friends? It's unnatural, sir…'

'And Clever Dick just dismissed the case on the spot.'

Horse grinned: 'And what did granny say?'

Kane smiled: 'I am happy to report, Mr Horse, that granny Fordyce was lost in the throng in the great Parliament Hall, by all accounts trying to pick a fight with one of the statues.'

Master and man laughed. 'And the last I saw of the now-confirmed Mr and Mrs Joseph Blakemore, I swear that they were both giggling like playmates and vowing to visit Mr Thin's bookshop to purchase the latest instalment of 'Bleak House'.'

'And what about money, sir?'

'No fee, Mr Horse.'

The manservant let out an involuntary - but clearly audible - groan.

Kane smiled: 'Nil desperandum, Mr Horse! Tomorrow sees the final instalment of our Russian novel - and I guarantee: we will not be paid in roubles…. '

*****

Chapter Fifteen

A Merry Heart

Barrowman, the solicitor for the Russian, consulted his pocket watch, 'Apologies, gentlemen - Mr Lermontov is not usually late.'

The police office at St Giles had a different air about it this time. On the one hand, the (current) absence of the truculent Russian had led to a more relaxed atmosphere among a group of people who knew each other well and were engaging now in a more informal form of chat.

On the other hand, Mackintosh of the Detective did seem distracted. The tardiness of the self-confessed killer had delayed a number of questions that had been troubling the detective's mind. Unanswered questions were always a form of torture to Mackintosh. Always disturbing his peace, like an angry teapot whistling to be taken off the fire.

Sergeant Wilson came into the room: 'We have a visitor, detective.'

Solicitor, Barrowman stood up: 'I told you, gentlemen, Mr Lermontov is…'

But it wasn't the Russian. The figure that was led in was the solicitor's clerk, a gawky, gangly youth named 'Sharkey'. Barrowman, the lad's employer was perplexed: 'Sharkey what in heaven's name…'

The boy took off his cap: 'Begging your pardon, Mr Barrowman. I thought I'd bring you up today's mail, sir, because…'

The solicitor snatched the letters: 'Give me those.' He tossed them onto the table. 'It's not correspondence we need - it's the Russian. This is akin to an emergency. Get yourself down to the New Club and fetch our client immediately.' He fumbled in his pocket and produced a coin. 'Here's half a crown - take a cab there and back if you must - but hurry, boy, hurry.' He waved the lad away. Sharkey gave the gentlemen a quick nod, put on his cap and ran out of the door. The solicitor sat down, embarrassed: 'Apologies, gentlemen. My wife's nephew. The boy's an idiot.'

They sat in silence for a time, then Mackintosh produced a sheaf of papers from the drawer of his desk. He then produced his notebook from his pocket. 'While we're waiting for your client to appear, gentlemen. I wonder if we could clarify a few matters. It shouldn't take too long.' Barrowman and Edward Kane leaned forward.

'Now, when Mr Kane here asked Mr Lermontov what he did right after disposing of the unfortunate architect, George Meikle Kemp…'. He nodded towards Kane, who smiled back in acknowledgement, '…your client responded that he looked up at the full moon and the stars and such.'

'Yes?'

'Well, I've checked the almanacs and newspapers and such for that date, sir. And there was no full moon that night.

The solicitor considered this: 'An air of theatricality perhaps in the telling of the tale. You've seen for yourself what Mr Lermontov is like…'

The detective continued: 'And as far as looking down into the water is concerned, I've consulted with Sergeant Wilson - he was there that night - and he says that the fog was so thick, he could hardly see his hand in front of him - never mind, seeing a hat and such floating in the water.'

The solicitor sighed: 'These are points that we can raise with my client when he gets here.' He took a piece of paper from his case and began to write. 'I will make a list of your questions.'

Mackintosh nodded: 'You can add this, then. Mr Lermontov says that he arrived at Leith Docks and - more or less immediately - sought out Kemp.'

'That is my understanding, yes.'

The detective leaned back in his chair: 'I took the liberty of consulting the Register of the Harbour Master for that date. There was no mention of any 'Lermontov' on any ship manifest, whether either passenger or crew.'

Barrowman looked up from his paper. Were those beads of sweat forming on his brow? The solicitor coughed: 'No doubt, travelling incognito - given that he was in possession of so much money in those suitcases. Most likely, he did not want to attract attention to his true identity as a Russian nobleman.'

The detective pressed on: 'And you recall, sir, your client insisting that he had struck Kemp with that rolled-up plan of the old church. The one that was written in Dutch. Difficult to make out…'

Barrowman sat back in his chair: 'You will agree with me, detective, that account was vivid and had the ring of truth about it.'

'Well, when I had people look at it, sir, it seems that the entry printed at the end of the scroll - 'mrt45' - is the date it was made…'

'Yes?'

'…and from the Dutch, translates into March 1845 - some 12 months after the alleged murder…' Mackintosh looked up from his notes, inviting an answer.

Barrowman began to stutter: 'I'm sure that there is some reasonable…'

Mackintosh marched on. He reached into the drawer of his desk and produced a black notebook. The notebook that had been handed over by the Russian to confirm his guilt: 'And this. We only got this back late on last night.'

Barrowman pointed over: 'Of course - Mr Lermontov's detailed account of the regrettable events. Unfortunately, entirely in the Russian language.'

The detective nodded: 'Correct, sir. Correct about the language. Pity about the account. When it was looked over by our people, turns out that it's just a lot of old poetry. Yes - by a chap called Lermontov - but that particular fellow appears to have died some ten years ago. Which begs the question, sir - who exactly is YOUR fellow?'

Barrowman was floundering now: 'I…I…'

The solicitor's struggle was interrupted by the entrance of Desk Sergeant Wilson: 'The boy is back sir - the one sent to the New Club.' Enter an out-of-breath Sharkey: 'Mr Barrowman - I took a cab like you said. Except I had a disagreement with the driver about the fare. He said…'

Barrowman raised his hand to halt the narrative: 'Not that, Sharkey, forget that. Where is Lermontov?'

'I went to the New Club like you asked sir and asked for him. They led me up to his rooms, but there was no answer at the door. So I told them - as you said, sir, that his kin had an emergency - so they unlocked the rooms.'

The boy stopped, to catch his breath. The solicitor waved his hands: 'And?'

'No sign, sir. They hadn't seen him for days. Last thing he said was that he might go to Glasgow. And - I'm telling you, sir, that room - it was was a right cowp!

The solicitor sat in stunned silence. Then the boy added: 'Oh - and they said that they'd be sending you the bill for the room and the food and all the wine and the damage an' all, sir.'

Barrowman looked around and tried to put on a brave face: 'Well, at least we have the expenses covered. A considerable sum in roubles lodged with the Bank of England.'

'That'll be in that letter, sir.' Sharkey nodded towards the letters that had been tossed onto the table: 'Like I was trying to tell you…'

Barrowman was still for a moment, then, in a frenzied motion, seized on the pile and scrambled through the letters until he produced one clearly marked 'Bank of England'. He ripped it open and scanned it. Then, an apparent moment of calm as he deliberately placed the letter back into its envelope. He did not speak for a time. Then: 'They have never heard of Lermontov. Their letter of comfort was a forgery. Oh - and all of those paper roubles – they were counterfeit too…'

*****

Mr Horse drank from his tin cup and rubbed his stubbly chin: 'So if the Russian bloke was a con man, then how come he was throwing all that money about, sir?'

Kane sipped his tea by the fire: 'It wasn't his money, Horse. The solicitors thought that those suitcases of roubles had put them in funds, so they gave him their own letter of comfort and he was able to pledge their credit wherever he went. And, by golly, he did just that. They reckon that he must have spent over a hundred pounds…'

'And what about us, sir? Did we get paid at all?'

'Nothing, Mr Horse. I say 'nothing' - except those two items I brought home this morning. Tendered by a flustered and embarrassed solicitor. What appears to be a bottle of fine malt whisky - no doubt given to him by some grateful - and authentic - client. And that small envelope containing some counterfeit Russian roubles. Offered, I suppose, as a kind of souvenir.'

Horse grinned: 'Well here's the thing, Mr K. I took them roubles out with me later. And I knows a bloke what knows a bloke…' He winked and tapped his nose, '… if you catch my drift. And he looks through them and I can see him getting excited. So he says that he'll take them off my hands…'

'And?'

The manservant reached into his pocket and produced notes and coins. He put them on the table: 'Three pound, seventeen and six, sir.'

Kane sat wide-eyed: 'I can only to imagine the sheer number of offences committed in that single transaction - but thank you, Horse. Thank you!'

The manservant began to scowl: 'But, Mr K, you know that bottle of fine whisky the lawyer gave you?'

'Yes?'

Horse shook his head: 'Some bad news, sir…'

'In what respect?'

'Well, I had a thought this morning: bad things usually come in threes, don't they?'

Kane shrugged: 'I'm not quite catching your drift, Mr Horse'

'Bad things. And things being fake, and the like sir. Come in threes, don't they.' He counted on his fingers: 'You got the fake Russian - number one…'

'Yes…'

'And then the fake husband what come back from India - number two…'

'Mr Horse – I'm not sure…'

'Oh, that bloke was a fake, sir.' He pointed at his master for emphasis: 'Dogs don't lie – they don't, Mr K! So I thought: 'Is the number three fake going to be that bottle of whisky' - must be worth a right few bob - and who would give that away? Just too good to be true. And, I'm telling you, that seal on the bottle looked wery dodgy to me. So I opened it. And would you believe it…'

Kane closed his eyes and expected the worst: 'Yes?'

Horse smiled. 'It was real…sir. By jingo, Mr K- it was WERY real!' He smacked his lips together.

The Advocate opened his eyes: 'So what was the bad news about the whisky?'

'The bad news, sir, is that I had to break the seal, so we can't sell it now, can we? You know what that means.'

The young Advocate smiled in spite of himself: 'Enlighten me, Mr Horse…'

'That means that we're going to have to drink it ourselves, ain't we? Now, I've just washed us a couple of tumblers, sir. And we can have a nip.'

Horse took the bottle of fine malt whisky and poured two significant measures into the tumblers. His master took a sip. He raised his eyebrows and smiled: 'You were not wrong, Mr Horse. This is very fine whisky indeed.'

The manservant raised his glass: 'Cheers, Mr K.'

The young Advocate sat back in his chair nursing his glass. He smiled: 'Thank you, Mr Horse. For that three pounds, seventeen and sixpence.' He sighed: 'And things will improve – I'm certain of it.' He raised his glass: 'Above all, we must remain cheerful.'

'I do me best, sir.'

Kane smiled: 'My father was a clergyman, you know that….'

The manservant gave a little chuckle: 'You may have mentioned it the odd hundred times, sir.'

'And he used to quote from…I think it was Proverbs…'A merry heart is like good medicine.' Kane raised his glass again: 'I will now propose a toast, Mr Horse. In the last twenty-four hours, we appeared to have survived a fake husband, fake roubles and a very real swine of a judge, and yet we remain cheerful. 'A merry heart is like good medicine'. A toast, then, my friend: Here's to a merry heart!'

Horse held up his glass of fine whisky and winked: 'And here's to more medicine...

*****

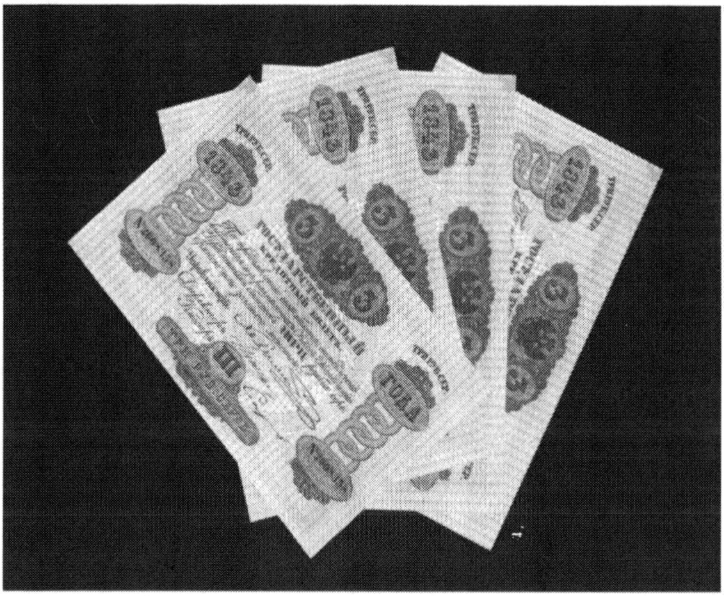

Edward Kane

and

The Supernal Sisters (2023)

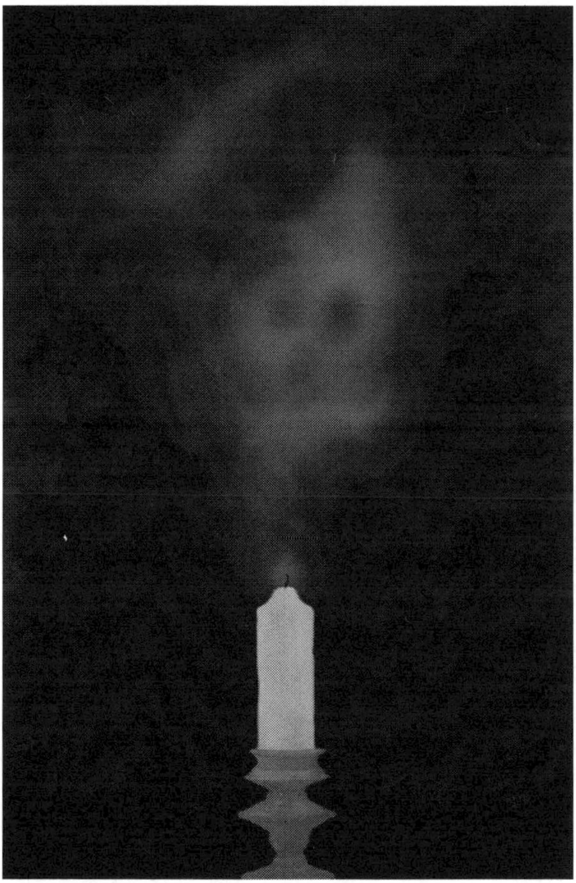

Chapter One

'Jesus Was Just Like a Ghost'

Edinburgh 1853

They might not have admitted it, but the men around the table were terrified. Understandable, perhaps, since this was an attempt to communicate with the dead.

Sarah Spooner - Spirit Medium - began to speak in a low, croaky (and in what sounded like) long-dead voice: 'Oh, my son, my son…'

The well-dressed man in his twenties sitting across the table (presumably the 'my son' referred to in the communication) placed his hands to his temple. This action made the medium snap out of her trance and - like an angry school-mistress - point over at the young gentleman: 'Hands! Hands!'. The fellow put his hands back down and interlocked them with the others around the circular table. Spooner sat back and closed her eyes. Croaky voice again: 'My son…why have you not avenged…my death?'

The young fellow sat still. But was that a tear running down his cheek?

*****

Edinburgh. The Old Town.

'Do you believe in ghosts, Mr K?'

Edward Kane, Advocate was rather caught on the hop by the question.

It was breakfast time. Kane's Cockney manservant, Mr Horse, had already performed near-Biblical miracles in securing for that impecunious household (what he had assured his master was) 'a nice bit of bacon'.

That last piece of breakfast was poised to enter the master's mouth, but the act of inserting it was now frozen in mid-air. It seemed to Kane impolite to complete the action now that he had been asked the direct question.

Mr Horse chuckled and pointed to the young Advocate: 'Sorry, Mr K - I put you off your stride. I was just wondering, like.' He nodded towards the poised fork hovering at his master's mouth: 'Get that breakfast down you - while it's hot, sir.'

The manservant, sitting on his low stool by the open fire, went back to toasting the large heel of some day-old bread, holding the darkening surface against the flames with the safe distance of a long fork.

Kane resumed the completion of his breakfast. He then took a sip of tea and considered the question. 'Ghosts? Why do you ask, Mr Horse?'

'Just wondering. I've been talking to some people down the Doric Tavern. And you always know all about this stuff, about The Bible and all…'

The young Advocate gave a little chuckle: 'I'm not sure what The Bible has to do with ghosts, Mr Horse.'

The manservant rubbed his stubbly chin: 'Me old nan used to say that Jesus was just like a ghost when he was walking on the water, sir.'

Kane sipped his tea. 'Certainly, his men thought he was one during the storm, but he soon disabused them of that.' He nodded towards the blackening bread on the flames: 'Now, I wonder if we could leave the topic of 'ghost' and focus on the issue of 'toast'.'

Horse blew out the now-flaming piece of bread, walked across and plonked the toast onto his master's side-plate: 'Wery droll, Mr K, Wery droll. I'll just lay out your things…'

*****

'I'm worried about my man, Horse.'

'I've met him. You ought to be…'

Edward Kane and his friend and colleague, Collins, were sipping their morning coffee in the Reading Room in the Advocates Library.

Easy chairs, pipe smoke, newspapers and coffee.

Kane placed his cup onto its saucer: 'My man appeared to be obsessed with the after-life this morning. Kept asking me about ghosts in The Bible…'

Collins frowned: 'Are there any?'

This type of Biblical inquisition (apparently now from all directions) was not unusual. Kane's late father had been a Church of Scotland minister. One of Kane's earliest memories was being dressed in his Sunday best, sitting on his mother's lap in church, and hearing one of his father's sermons. That was the first of, perhaps, thousands of homilies to which the young Advocate had been exposed throughout his childhood, his teen years then early adulthood. His father had joked that Edward's residual knowledge of the Bible would ultimately resemble the ring of dirt left in a bath-tub after an extremely long soak.

Kane sat back in his chair and considered the question. Ghosts in the Bible? His manservant's example came to mind: 'I suppose when Jesus' men saw him walking on the water, they became alarmed because they thought that he was ghost…'

Collins pushed his horn-rim spectacles against the bridge of his nose: 'And didn't the good Lord actually conduct a seance at one point?'

Kane frowned: 'A seance??? I think not, my friend. If you mean 'Lazarus', then…'

Collins sat forward: 'No, no - he did. Near the end. Jesus went up a hill and he had a long conversation with Elijah and Moses. And those two chaps must have been well dead by then.' The friends laughed.

Collins took off his glasses, fished out a little piece of silk from his waistcoat pocket and began to polish the lenses: 'It always reminded me of the appeal court here, when our three judges go into a sort of holy huddle against the back wall before they hand down their decision.'

Kane smiled: 'As always, you are, of course, right, Collins.' He thought for a moment, then: 'Although, I think that Elijah was never recorded as dead. Carried away by a tornado straight up to heaven, as I recall.'

Collins raised his teacup: 'Well, if you see him - give him my best…'

The friends laughed and sipped their tea.

Collins gave a chuckle and sat back in his chair: 'So what does today hold for that illustrious young Advocate, Edward Kane, my friend?'

A shake of the head: 'If you were to substitute the word 'impecunious' for the word 'illustrious', then I would answer to that, Collins.' Kane took his Hunter out of his waistcoat pocket and studied its face: 'Although, in some forty-five minutes, I am due to consult.'

'About what?'

Kane laughed: 'I have absolutely no idea. Don't even know the client's name. Just a very odd letter of instruction. The whole thing is a mystery.'

Kane reached into his briefcase and produced an envelope. He handed it to his friend. Without opening it, Collins took the envelope and held it under his nose. Kane furrowed his brows: 'Is it scented, my friend? I hadn't…' Collins gave a mischievous grin: 'No Edward. It just struck me from the quality of the paper that these instructions have the distinct aroma of a very, very wealthy client…' The friends laughed and Collins continued: 'Now – let's see what's in it, shall we?'

*****

Chapter Two

Subterranean Provision

The Advocates Library. The Reading Room.

Collins sipped his tea and began to open the letter: 'Curious. Very curious. And who are the instructing agents?'

'The instructing solicitors are a firm called 'Abernathy and Hawkes' - I can't say that I've ever heard of them…'

At his point, Collins spluttered in his tea. Kane leaned in: 'I'm sorry, my friend, what did I….?'

Collins coughed a little, wiped his mouth with his handkerchief, then regained his composure: 'Edward, 'Abernathy and Hawkes' are…I struggle to describe them…let us just say that this is a legal firm with very few clients, and each client tends to be a member of the aristocracy. Or rich beyond the dreams of avarice. Are you sure that there is no clue in that letter of instruction?' He removed the letter from the envelope and read it through, nodding as he went. He placed the letter back in the envelope and handed it back: 'You are correct, my friend. No client. No subject heading. Nothing. The whole thing remains a mystery. But I suspect, Edward, that what you hold in your hand,' he nodded towards the letter, 'is not so much a letter of instruction as the entrance to an Aladdin's cave of treasure…'

*****

'Snuff, Mr Kane?'

'I beg your pardon?'

'A pinch of snuff, sir? Would you care for a pinch of snuff?'

Kane gave a weak smile: No thank you.'

They had been waiting for a good ten minutes now. No sign of any client.

Advocate and instructing solicitor sat in silence. Cameron Abernathy, solicitor, best described as large, round and hairless, began to whistle (somewhat tunelessly, it must be said) and to drum his fingers on the table in no discernible rhythm.

Kane studied the gold snuff box on the highly-polished table in the consultation rooms of Abernathy and Hawkes. Immediately there had been something about these offices that had made the young Advocate supremely uncomfortable. Just something about the place. It reeked of...what was it? Of money. Yes, money. Of course, that, of itself, was not bad. It was just that this was the kind of lawyer's firm (according to Collins) where merchant bankers would come and make subterranean provision for children born out of wedlock from illicit trysts with social inferiors. Where the nobility would consult about some dark secret, usually some harmful act that was to be swept under the carpet by the use of their position and money. Failing which, intimidation where the problem would be escorted out of the royal door - like a beggar by burly footmen - shooed away by the threat of disgrace and ruinous legal proceedings.

As they sat in silence, Kane mused that this was not why he had become a lawyer. He has become a lawyer to do good! They waited. And waited. Kane's mind began to wander. The Advocates Library stored not just legal books, but many treasures. Among those was the Flodden Flag. The banner that had been unfurled by the Scots in battle in 1513. And the flag trumpeted: 'Veritas Vincit' - 'The truth wins'. Kane gave an inward groan. In the little time he had spent as an Advocate, he had soon realised that the truth was the last thing that most litigants wanted to hear and was often the first casualty on the battlefield of court proceedings.

The profusely sweating solicitor, Abernathy, took his timepiece from his pocket and shook his head. He reminded Kane of a nervous pig in a butcher's shop. Abernathy looked up: 'You're probably wondering what this whole thing is about, Mr Kane.'

Kane - ever polite - nodded with a smile: 'Your letter of instruction was…commendably brief, Mr Abernathy.'

'It's the client, Mr Kane. Absolute discretion is assured. You understand…'

'Of course.'

The solicitor leaned in: 'But while we wait for the client, sir, I wonder if I might ask you a question?'

'Of course. Anything.

'Do you…um…do you…'. The solicitor gave a little cough, '…do you have any experience of…of exhuming a dead body?'

*****

The door flew open. Two people came in. Only one was in any kind of a hurry. That would be the other partner in the firm of Abernathy and Hawkes: John Hawkes. In contrast to the expansive, rolling plains of the bald Mr Abernathy, Mr Hawes was reminiscent of an over-excited, hairy maypole.

The other party entering - the one for whom the words 'in a hurry' could never apply - was a man in his mid-twenties, Harry Humbie. Son of Alexander Humbie.

Some people are immediately dis-likeable. Harry Humbie was such a person. A life of privilege had engendered in him a general air of disdain. He would roll his languid superiority into every room as a child might roll in a hoop and a stick.

It was Humbie's father and grandfather who had amassed the family fortune. In Fish. Barrels and barrels of fish meant barrels and barrels of money. First selling from a barrow, then door-to-door, then owning shops, then a factory, then factories (plural) - the accumulation of all that wealth over two generations from the sweat of their brow and the fruits of the sea. This rise-at-dawn and late-to-bed family work ethic, however, was not one that Harry Humbie appeared to have inherited. His father, Alexander, had always longed for his only son to be a gentleman. And the right amount of money lavished in the right places, coupled with the right (and expensive) education had, on the face of it, achieved this. Given his conspicuous wealth, the father, Alexander Humbie, had managed to marry above his station, bagging the fifth (and until that point entirely un-marriageable) daughter of a near-ruined aristocrat. By an uncanny coincidence, the sizeable dowry provided by Humbie was able to settle the gambling debts of the father of the bride, averting social disgrace. But, as Edward Kane was about to find out, Alexander Humbie's son, Harry, appeared to have inherited all of the wrong traits.

*****

Chapter Three

A Distasteful Joke

There was something of a distasteful joke in the Humbie family. Father, Alexander Humbie had come to harm as a child. One busy Saturday, as he was crossing the crowded streets of the Lawn Market, he was trampled by a passing horse and cart. Pain - yes. Tears - of course. But, nonetheless, the young Alexander - aged 10 - proceeded to make the delivery on time. It was only later that evening, when the pain had become unbearable for the lad, that the doctor required to be sent for. Arrived, shook his head - and promptly amputated the child's left pinkie toe. The joke was that they ought to employ that same horse to drag the son, Harry Humbie, out of bed in the morning. Then, as the boy grew, it was sometimes noted (in whispers) that the boy Harry began to treat his father with a measure of distain. Superiority laced with a touch of mild disgust. Like a wealthy Gentleman might treat a jobbing Tradesman.

In the consulting rooms of Abernathy and Hawkes, introductions were effected with a number of small bows and the shake of the young man's (limp and uninterested) hand then the two solicitors, the Advocate and the client finally sat around the table. Down to business. Hawkes, in contrast to his somewhat languid partner, was immediately animated and insistent:

'First, Mr Kane, apologies for any delay. Our client required to be...required to be....'

The young Harry interrupted: 'Don't beat about the bush, Hawkes - I was asleep. Had quite forgotten about this ridiculous little affair today…'

Kane thought to himself: …a 'ridiculous little affair'…involving a rich man, two partners of a law firm and an Advocate - what an odd way to begin a consultation…

Hawkes looked up: 'You're probably wondering why we have instructed you in particular, Mr Kane?' Hawkes gave a nervous smile, then realised that he had been somewhat gauche: 'Oh, I do hope you take no offence from my comment, sir?'

Kane returned the smile. (He had wondered the same thing himself as he walked into those plush offices). The Advocate gave a little nod to indicate that Hawkes should proceed.

The solicitor stumbled a little at first, but soon warmed to his task: 'You see, the situation…the situation is somewhat delicate and Mr Humbie here,' he nodded over to the client (who did not look too engaged), 'he has something of a social standing. And if we were to instruct, say, the Dean of Faculty or perhaps an Advocate of superior rank, then the word might spread that…'

Kane held up his hand to indicate that the solicitor did not have to explain further. In plain words, this entitled young man across the table wanted to raise something with the courts and did not want anyone in his social circle - the Dean of Faculty or perhaps those school friends called to the Bar - to be alerted to his folly. Kane could almost see them guffawing around the dinner table in Drummond Place. Better to instruct a person of no great social standing who did not travel in those rarefied circles. Who better than an impoverished Son of the Manse with no social cachet at all? Who better than struggling young Advocate, Edward Kane?

Hawkes reached into his briefcase and produced a piece of paper: 'You will forgive me, Mr Kane, for the cloak of secrecy here, but I have prepared - by my own hand - a short Memorandum for you and I did not want to leave this in public, sir - even in an Advocate's box.'

He handed the paper over to Kane: 'And I should be grateful if you could hand it back when finished. By all means, make your own notes, but even in those, please leave out of account anything that might identify the parties.'

Kane took the paper and began to study it. Then he looked up to see Hawkes offering an engraved golden box: 'Snuff, Mr Kane?'

*****

Despite the circumlocution with which the legal problem had been expressed on paper (understandable, since, after all, lawyers were paid by the word) the sense of the situation soon became clear. The languid young man's father - Alexander Humbie - had suffered an unexpected death. He had been travelling by coach from Edinburgh to Glasgow on a last-minute business mission when he was taken ill. He complained that he had double vision and that he was feeling extremely confused. This was unusual for a man normally as fit as he was. The coachman stopped at a post house at Falkirk and took the ailing fish magnate inside to see if anything could be done. While outside the coach house, the coach - and its remaining passengers - fell prey to a gang of robbers. The robbers took everything of value from the coach and the passengers: rings, gold watches, necklaces, engraved walking sticks and - most importantly in this case - the manifest containing the names and details of those travelling. Alexander Humbie fell asleep in that coach house and never woke up again. He died alone. No-one knew who he was. The manifest containing his name had been stolen. Also, there was no record of him in the Edinburgh office, Humbie being the last-minute passenger on the coach. The body lay unclaimed in the coach house for two days and then - as was permitted by the 1832 Anatomy Act – was duly certificated as an unclaimed body, then taken to the Anatomy Rooms of Edinburgh University for dissection, where the anonymous body of Alexander Humbie - fish magnate - was gutted before an invited room of students and paying guests.

Kane looked up and was suddenly conscious that the lawyers and the client were studying him. He looked towards the son, Harry Humbie: 'My commiserations, Mr Humbie. It must have been of great distress to you to lose your father in such a fashion. Especially…'

The young man shrugged, said nothing and looked towards the window. Hawkes, the solicitor, filled the silence: 'Mr Kane, sir, now that you have been apprised of the circumstances, you will be wondering what your part of this affair might entail.'

Kane nodded. Although - in truth - the young Advocate had been so engrossed in the reading of the tale of the unfortunate Alexander Humbie that he had, for a time, forgotten why he was there. Not only that, but there was now the faint beginning of an awful headache.

Hawkes continued: 'You see, when the body of the unfortunate Alexander Humbie was, um…' (in deference to the sensitivities of the deceased's only son sitting across the table, he was reluctant to say the word 'dissected') '…when the body was examined. Our client informs us that it was found to contain a considerable quantity of arsenic.'

It was only now that the client spoke: 'My father was poisoned, Mr Kane. He must have been. Probably by a jealous rival.'

Kane sat back in his chair and tried not to show his surprise: 'And what makes you think that, sir? That your father was poisoned.'

'Because I was told.'

'By whom?'

'By my dead father, Mr Kane. By my dead father…'

*****

Chapter Four

A Colourable Reason?

Back in the cramped (but suitably inexpensive) lodgings in the Edinburgh Old Town, manservant, Mr Horse couldn't help but laugh: '…and when you get to court, Mr K, you can get that old dead father out of the coffin and into the witness box and the judge will start shouting at you: 'And where did you dig him up, Mr Kane. Where did you dig him up?" Horse continued to laugh for a long time at his own joke and brushed away the tears of laughter with his sleeve. 'Honestly, sir, sometimes you talk such a load of gammon and spinach…'

Kane sat in his wing-back chair by the fire, nursing his glass of rum and milk: 'Not me, Mr Horse. It's the client. He says that he was taken by a friend to see a spirit medium - a 'Miss Spooner' - and that lady gave him the message from his father from beyond the grave.'

Horse frowned: 'I heard of the lady, Mr K. My little friend, Maisie, you know - the one what sometimes does a shift down at the Doric Tavern…'

(Kane nodded. But in truth he had not remembered this particular lady's name since his manservant Mr Horse appeared to have more than a passing acquaintance with every barmaid in Edinburgh.)

Horse continued: …well, the thing about Maisie is that she is a woman of many talents. Not only does she pull a decent glass of beer, but she has a nice sideline in dressing bodies.'

"'Dressing bodies'?'

Horse nodded: 'You know - when some geezer snuffs it and they want to put him out on the table in the parlour for the night before they send him off to the graveyard…'

'Yes?'

'Well, they don't want him looking like a tramp, do they? So, they get Maisie in and she gets makeup and such on them and gets them dressed into their Sunday best so that they can receive visitors and the like.'

Kane smiled: 'I don't expect the conversation will be too scintillating, though…'

'If I had any idea what you was taking about, Mr K, then I wager that would be wery amusing, but…' the manservant stroked his stubbly chin: '…here's the thing: Maisie said that one of the families that she done the business for, their old uncle had died and they was trying to figure out what jacket the old dead uncle wanted - in the coffin, like - and they couldn't agree, so they went to see Miss Spooner…'

'The spirit medium…'

Horse nodded. 'The spirit medium sir. And she got in touch with the old bloke - on the other side - and so they got it from the horse's mouth, so to speak.'

Kane shook his head: 'What a curious business!'

'Oh, it's all the rage, sir. All the best people are doing it.' Horse leaned forward. 'And in case you're wondering,

Mr K, the old uncle plumped for the smoking jacket. And wery spruce he felt in it an' all. At least, that what he told them…'

*****

'Experience? Of exhuming a dead body?' Collins shook his head. 'I fear that I cannot help you with that, my friend.'

Kane blew air from his cheeks. 'Apparently, I would require permission from the Sheriff Substitute before this could be done. What's needed, as I understand it, would be a colourable reason for doing so.'

Collins sat back in his chair and pondered the question: 'You will forgive me, Edward, for asking an indelicate question.'

'Yes?'

'But after the dissection itself, what becomes of the organs that are removed? Are they then re-inserted, post-mortem - rather like stuffing a Christmas turkey - or are they preserved in aspic or the like, or…'. (At this point, Collins gave a small shake of the head to indicate that he had run out of options).

Kane pondered this: 'I confess, I have no idea…'

Collins leaned forward: 'Then time to find out, I wager. The whole event is relatively recent. Speak to the anatomist. It will be a professor at the university. No doubt he - and a number of keen students - will have taken detailed notes from the event.'

Kane frowned: 'And what will that achieve?'

'Two things. One: a better understanding into the mechanism of death and the possibility - however remote - of foul play in the eminent fishmonger's demise.'

Kane nodded: 'And 'two'?'

Collins smiled: "Two': the conversation will be billed as a 'consultation'. And will attract a healthy fee…'

*****

Edinburgh University. The Old College

'What did you say your name was?'

'Hawkes, sir, John Hawkes of the firm Abernathy and Hawkes.'

'Never heard of you.' The professor pointed to the young Advocate standing beside the solicitor: 'And who is this? Your apprentice?'

'This is Mr Kane the Advocate, sir.'

'The Advocate???' William Peterson, FRSE FRCSE, Professor of Anatomy at the University of Edinburgh adjusted his pince-nez and studied the two figures standing hat-in-hand before him. He sighed: 'Well, I suppose you had better come in then.'

Much patting of waistcoats and fumbling in pockets before the good professor finally bent down, reached into his case and produced a large key that he placed into the lock. Door opened, the academic led the lawyers into his chambers. Kane looked around. It looked as though a tornado had entered the room and had swept the books from their shelves, scattering them around the room. The walls may have been adorned with beautiful pastoral pictures, but these were largely covered by large, crudely-drawn illustrations of skeletons and cut-away attempts at drawing the musculature of the human body.

The professor motioned to a stack of chairs in the corner: 'Sit down, won't you…'

Kane moved to lift a pile of books off one of the chairs, but was immediately halted as the professor held up a prohibitive hand: 'No - not that one!'

Professor Peterson then walked around the room studying each book-laden chair, examining them as if they were soldiers on parade. He placed the books onto the floor then pointed: 'This one.' Another inspection, then: 'And this one.'

Kane and his instructing solicitor lifted up the designated chairs and drew them towards the professorial desk. Professor Peterson was already seated and stuffing a pipe with tobacco. After a struggle with some tobacco that refused to be lit, the academic gave a few contented puffs of the pipe and smiled over the desk: 'So gentlemen - before we begin, let me just say: I know why you are here.'

Hawkes frowned: 'You do, sir?'

'Of course,' - *puff* *puff* - 'men of your rank and calibre - it is plain as a pikestaff. I am not stupid, gentlemen…'

*****

Chapter Five

A Much Sought-After Dresser of the Dead

The Doric Tavern was quiet at this time of day. Mr Horse nursed his jug of foamy beer as he listened to Maisie Mount (sometime Doric barmaid and much-sought-after Dresser of the Dead).

'I'm telling ye, Horse - they two lassies - that medium wifie and her sister – oooh - they give me the right creeps,'

Maisie nodded to the manservant's drink: 'Give me that.' Horse handed over his near-finished jug. Maisie looked around to make sure that she wasn't being watched. Then pulled the pump and filled up Horse's drink. She gave him a sly wink and handed it back. 'That one is on the house for - you know - 'old lang syne' and that…'

Horse gave a sly wink and held up the drink in toast to his bonny benefactor: '…and a bit more of the 'old acquaintance' when you get off.'

The barmaid laughed: 'Who you calling 'old'??? Ye cheeky scamp.' She mock-reached over to take back the beer.

Horse smiled and held the jug to himself: 'It's a 'cup of kindness', darlin' - don't forget that!' They laughed. Horse took a deep drink and wiped his mouth with his sleeve: 'You do pull a proper glass of beer, Maisie. So – as I was saying – my master, Mr Kane was telling me about one of his clients went to see them sisters – ended up speaking to his old dead dad on the other side and the old bloke says he was done in - with the arsenic.'

Maisie nodded, lifted up a rag and polished a glass as she spoke: 'You hear all sorts of things in that room. Sounds about right. There's two of them. Sisters, I mean. Sarah Spooner and Sukie Spooner. One of them is the medium - that's 'Sarah' - she's the one that talks to the spirits. She does the voices and that.' Maisie dipped her head and made imitation of the medium in a low voice: "I am yer deid faither. I know why youse are here. I never hid the money you're looking for - I went and spent it. Oh, and yer Aunty Fanny is on the other side an' all and she says 'Hello'..."

Horse spluttered a laugh into his beer. Maisie continued: 'And then there's the wee sister, 'Susan' - but folk call her 'Sukie' - she, like, helps the medium sister out. She lets you into the house and lays out the chairs and such. But she's a real dark horse, that one. Sometimes you look across that table and the wee sister is in a trance an' all'. They're a right pair, they two.'

Horse grinned: 'Sounds like the magician at a fair and his lovely assistant.'

Maisie was suddenly serious: 'But this is no' like pulling a coin out of your lug, Horse, or pulling a chicken out of a hat. I'm telling you. I've seen things at these meetings. Real things. These sisters. They've gave themselves a name. 'The super…super..'. The barmaid shook her head. 'It's a word I don't know.' Maisie noted the concentrated look on Horse's face: 'And look at you, all serious. And all about women.' She polished the glass: 'That must be a first.'

Horse smiled: 'I was just thinking that I'd like to have a look at them…'

The barmaid had a gleam in her eye: : 'And did I mention that sister Sukie is a pretty wee package an' all? Very bonny.'

'In that case, my dear, I would very much like to have a look at them…'

Maisie flicked her rag at the grinning manservant and he gave a comical duck away from it. She shook her head and kept polishing: 'Well, you happen to be in luck, you cheeky midden. I'm going to one of their meetings tonight.'

'Tonight?'

'Some rich old wifie has passed away and - again - there's a stooshie in the family about what's she's to wear in the coffin. So they're going to see if they can get an answer from the old woman that's passed.'

Mr Horse frowned: 'But if you're there for the family, what am I meant to be doing there?'

Maisie winked: 'I'll be the magician, Horse, and you can be my lovely assistant.' She looked serious for a moment: 'Big problem for you, though.'

'What?'

'You're going to have to shave…'

*****

'I'm afraid that you appear to have the wrong end of the stick, Professor Peterson.'

John Hawkes, solicitor, sat in the professor's office, turning his hat in his hands as he sat. Peterson looked over the desk at Hawkes and Kane: 'Well, if you do not wish to purchase tickets for the upcoming dissection, then how may I help you, sirs?'

Hawkes quickly explained their mission: information concerning a recent autopsy - performed by Professor Peterson himself - where Alexander Humbie (millionaire fish magnate) had died unexpectedly, had been declared an unclaimed body and had been consigned to the Anatomy Rooms.

The professor listened, puffing on his pipe and nodding his head as the narrative unfolded. Finally, he took the pipe out of his mouth and tapped its bowl in the palm of his hand as he considered his response: 'I remember that one well, gentlemen. Gentleman in his fifties. It was difficult to establish cause of death with no surrounding information. With other cadavers it's often easy: the murderer cut down from the scaffold - I wager that I could narrate the story of their life from the newspaper reports alone without examining the body. Unclaimed bodies from hospitals - again, the admission papers from the ward will tell the tale - the age, occupation and so forth of the deceased. The post-mortem in such cases is an exercise in confirmation of what we already know, rather than an exploration of what we don't. But in the case of…of…what was his name again…bear with me…'

'Alexander Humbie.'

With that, the professor put his pipe back in his mouth, got up from his desk and walked over and peered at a pile of papers in the corner: 'Of course. What date did you say?'

Hawkes confirmed the date from his notes and the professor ran his finger down the stacked papers. He pulled out a sheaf of papers and went through them: 'Ah, yes - here it is. The Fish Man - as we later discovered once he was safely buried - one 'Alexander Humbie' - but we weren't to know the identity at the time. One of five autopsies. A good haul for that session.' He gave a little chuckle: 'And the esteemed Mr Humbie was not the freshest catch of the day, I'm bound to say.' Professor Peterson was soon engrossed in the papers and mumbling to himself: 'Umm…yes…mmm…. I see…'. He looked up, took the piece of paper and patted it against his other hand. Hawkes and Kane saw what looked like bloodstains on it.

Edward Kane - who had so far said little - ventured a question: 'It is our understanding that there may have been some question of…of…how shall I put it…um…poison?'

The professor studied the young Advocate's face for a moment. Then burst into uncontrolled laughter.

*****

Chapter Six

Nothing More Than a Jumped-Up Fishmonger

Horse bristled: 'How much???'

The old lady doing the selling held up her hand: 'I don't ken what you're moaning about, Mr Horse.' She held up the disputed item. 'This scarf is made of pure silk. Did ye hear that, son - 'pure silk'!' She drew herself up to her full height: 'All the way frae China.'

'I don't mind paying for the scarf, dear, but I'll be blowed if I'm paying for its passage from China an' all.

The manservant had stood before Mrs McMeechan's little shop in Gladstone's Land for a good half hour now, examining the cravats and handkerchiefs that were hanging on a rope by the window and swaying in the breeze. The handkerchiefs in particular were of a very fine quality, no doubt snatched surreptitiously from their owners in the crowd on a busy Lawn Market Saturday and sold on to the old lady for pennies.

'Can you show me something cheaper?'

Mrs McAllister - increasingly frustrated - narrowed her eyes and examined Horse: 'Well, what is it for, son? A christening? A funeral?'

The manservant found himself struggling to explain that the evening's event was one where they would try to communicate with the dead.

'That's not your business, my dear - now I want to see something that's cheap.'

The old lady sighed: 'Have you looked in the mirror?'

*****

'Poison? Oh dear, oh dear…'

Professor Peterson stopped laughing, gave a rueful shake of the head and tapped his pipe on the wooden ashtray, emptying out the spent tobacco, and sighed: 'You've been speaking to the unfortunate fellow's son, haven't you.'

'How did you know?'

'When it came to light that the man on the slab had been his late father, the young son came to see - or should I say 'accost' - me out there on the quadrangle. Quite an objectionable young fella too.'

Hawkes and Kane looked at each other and nodded, but said nothing. The professor continued: 'I brought him in here and showed him my notes. The lad seemed obsessed by the fact that his father had a considerable quantity of quicksilver in his system…'

Kane frowned: 'Quicksilver? Wouldn't that explain…'

The professor was immediately dismissive: 'Oh - pish posh! The man on the dissection table was nothing more than a jumped-up fishmonger. He was always going to have raised levels of quicksilver. Mercury is a natural ingredient. It could have come from anywhere, especially fish. King mackerel, oysters - the little blighters are full of it.'

He struck a match on his desk and re-lit his pipe. He shook out the match. In his element now: 'People are always looking for a reason for death. That young fella certainly was. But the truth is simpler than that.' He picked up an hourglass that was sitting on his desk and turned it over. He watched the sand as it began to run: 'You are on this earth for a little time and then that time runs out. In truth, people drop dead all the time for no reason. The hourglass has simply run its course.' The professor looked up: 'And then 'clever' men like me are consulted and we give a name - a reason - for this most natural of events. And our guesses - educated guesses, yes, but still guesses - become the settled narrative in the matter.' He puffed on his pipe and chuckled: 'Sometimes I feel more akin to a novelist than a scientist.'

Silence in the room. Contented puffing on the pipe. The young Advocate broke the silence. He smiled: 'And what, if I may ask, was the educated guess in the case of Alexander Humbie?'

Professor Peterson leaned across. The desk: 'I'll tell you what it was not, sir. It was not a case of poisoning. But that young son – the one who importuned me in the quadrangle – he would have none of it. I mentioned the word 'mercury' and it lit him up like a fuse. Just looking for trouble.' He laughed: 'I tell you, gentlemen, I have seen more quicksilver in the bodies of those fellows taking Blue Mass pills for constipation!' He sucked on his pipe: 'No. This chap Alexander Humbie - his heart stopped beating while he was asleep. I've plumped for angina pectoris - an unfortunate bastardisation of the Latin and the Greek - meaning, I suppose 'a strangled chest'.

Professor Peterson stood up from his desk to indicate that the meeting was over: 'And so, gentlemen - you have my narrative. I am sorry that I could not...'

Edward Kane held up his hand: 'Forgive me, professor, I am extremely grateful, but a last question, if I might?'

Professor Peterson was far from happy. Took his Hunter from his waistcoat pocket and read the time. He sat down again and folded his hands on the desk, fingers inter-linked. A smile on his face, but not in his eyes: 'Yes?'

Kane asked: 'Do you think that the early childhood injury had any bearing on the final weakness in Mr Humbie's heart?'

The professor grimaced: 'The 'early childhood injury'? I am not quite following you, sir. What injury?'

'The injury to Mr Humbie's foot. When he was a child. The little toe of his...of his...'. Kane had forgotten which foot. He looked over at his instructing solicitor. Mr Hawkes jumped in: 'His left foot, sir. The 'pinkie' toe.' He made a cutting motion with his hands: 'Amputated. When the boy was ten.'

The Professor frowned as Kane resumed the question: 'I have heard it said, Professor Peterson, anecdotally, of course, that there appears to be some connection between the toes and the heart. And I was just wondering...'

This time it was the professor's turn to hush the Advocate. He held up his hand: 'You will forgive me this time, Mr...Mr...'. Solicitor Hawkes jumped in again: 'This is Mr Kane, the Advocate, professor. Peterson sat back in his chair: 'Well, 'Mr Kane the Advocate', I'm afraid that you have been mis-informed here. True: problems with the feet - notably, the toes - are sometimes on account of the heart not doing its job properly - not pumping enough blood down there, for example. But the feet- or more precisely - the absence of a toe - were not a a factor in this case. Mr Humbie had all of his toes, believe me. Had he been in any way digitally deficient, as you seem to think he was, then that would have been recorded in my notes. And look…' the professor held up his notes for examination by the visitors, '…no mention of such an issue here. Thus…'

Edward Kane sat back in his chair in silence. And had a startling thought.

*****

Chapter Seven

Almost Like a Real Gentleman

The young Advocate kept his thoughts to himself for now. Solicitor, John Hawkes, on the other hand, was respectful but vociferous: 'Professor Peterson, I'm afraid to say that Mr Kane is correct here. It was well-known - both in the family and in the wider Edinburgh community - that Alexander Humbie possessed only nine toes. He would sometimes walk with a slight limp and, latterly, required the use of a walking cane. Which cane was stolen when the coach in question was robbed, sir.'

Professor Peterson frowned: 'You are quite sure of this, Mr Hawkes?'

The solicitor smiled: 'I could not be more certain, sir.'

Peterson sat back in his chair again and studied his notes. Then he put the papers on the desk and began - absent-mindedly - to tap his failing pipe onto the wooden ashtray, obviously deep in thought.

tap *tap* *tap*

He nodded to himself. Then:

tap *tap* *tap*

Finally, Professor Peterson (FRSE FRCSE) re-surfaced and gave the gentlemen across the desk a warm smile.

'I am very grateful to you, gentlemen. You have assisted me in writing an entirely new chapter on the demise of that poor unclaimed creature on the dissection table. For it is now as plain as the nose on my face: the body that was on that table - and expertly examined by me was - without a doubt - dead. But – indisputably – it was not the body of fish magnate Alexander Humbie…'

*****

'Yer what, Mr K??? Not old Alexander Humbie?' Mr. Horse's eyes were wide in disbelief. 'If it weren't Alexander Humbie on that table, then who was it, sir?'

Edward Kane sat in his chair, cup of tea and side-plate of toast in his lap: 'They have no idea, Mr Horse. Apparently, there were five bodies brought to the university that day and there has obviously been an error when labelling their provenance.'

Horse frowned - not understanding the word. Kane clarified: 'A mistake when writing down where the body had come from.'

Horse gave a thumbs-up: 'So - what happened to the body of old Alexander, then?'

'The professor didn't know. He did only one of the autopsies that day and left the rest to junior colleagues. He said that he'd check to see if anyone else dealt with a body fitting Humbie's description in the other dissections that day.'

Mr Horse finished laying the table. Then went over to the open fire where a pot was cooking on the embers of the orange coals. He put a rag around the fingers of his left hand and lifted off the top of pot. Steam rose. Horse looked at the bubbling contents. He dipped his finger into the pot then quickly put it into his mouth. 'Oh, yes - that's a mighty good stew, Mr K. A bit salty, but then - that bit of mutton weren't born yesterday. I'll get you a bowl and you can dip yesterday's bread into it.'

Kane nodded. 'Thank you, Mr Horse.' He studied his manservant's face for a moment. It was covered in small cuts. 'And if you don't mind me asking - have you injured your face in some fashion?'

Horse rubbed his chin: 'No, sir. I've just had a shave…'

*****

Later that evening, the clean-shaven manservant and his occasional special friend, Maisie Mount, were knocking on the door of the residence of sisters, Sarah and 'Sukie' Spooner, spirt mediums who were encouraging adherents to use their preferred - and advertised - heavenly title 'The Supernal Sisters'. Horse stood at the front door and looked Maisie up and down: 'Have to say, Maisie - you do scrub up well, girl…'. Maisie tittered and gave a little curtsy. 'And you almost look like a real gentleman, Horsey. Remember - you're here to help me. That's the story. So keep your mouth shut and they won't know that you're really here to spy on them.'

Horse protested: 'I ain't no spy, Maisie.'

'Then you have no right to be here and you can just go home then, eh?'

Horse considered this for a moment: 'I'll keep me mouth shut…'

The door opened. And when it opened, Mr Horse was quite taken aback by the radiant vision of loveliness before him. Sukie Spooner, all warmth and smiles and petticoats and curls, welcomed Maise Mount like a long-lost friend. She took both of Maisie's hands: 'Why Miss Mount - delighted to have the pleasure of your company once again. Come in, come in.' Sukie nodded over to a lady's maid standing in the corner and the maid came over to take Maisie's coat. Sukie focused on Horse now. Still speaking to Maisie: 'And you have pleasured me…' (at this point that the expression caused some distraction in Horse) '…you have pleasured me with the company of this fine gentleman.' She smiled at Horse. 'I do not believe that we have had the pleasure, Mr…Mr…?'

Horse looked over at Maisie. He was reluctant to answer. They had agreed that he would stay silent as he posed as Maisie's assistant - but they hadn't thought of agreeing on a fake name for the introduction.

Maisie gave a brittle little smile: 'This is Mr…Mr…'. But her attempt at invention was frustrated by another voice. The voice was that of the lady's maid: 'Shall I take your coat, Mr Horse? The manservant looked up. The maid stood there, head slightly cocked, lips twisted into a malevolent smile. The maid repeated: 'Your coat. Mr Horse?'

*****

Chapter Eight

A Burning Ship and All That

Standing in the hallway of Suki and Spooner's house, Horse gave a little bow to the maid: ''Ello my dear.' A cautious glance. 'Bin a while ennit?' The detail came back to him. But slowly. 'Maggie', was it? Or, or 'Mildred'? Yes - Mildred. Mildred Morrison. She used to do a shift at The White Hart, then disappeared off the map. Story was that she had gone into service in one of the big houses. There was something about Mildred's nature that - despite her pleasing appearance - reminded Horse of curdled milk.

Sukie Spooner beamed: "Horse'? 'Mr Horse' - my goodness - what a charming name. And is that an English accent that I hear? And which part of that wonderful country do you come from, Mr Horse?'

'London, miss.'

Sukie's eyes widened: 'And from which part of that great metropolis do you hail, sir?'

'Bethnal Green, miss.

Sukie Spooner savoured the words like fine wine swirling around her palate: 'Ah - Bethnal Greeeen.' She beamed 'How lovely to be surrounded by nature.'

This was not how Mr Horse remembered Bethnal Green.

Sukie waved over to the maid: 'Mildred - won't you take the coats from our exotic guests.'

Horse helped Maisie off with her coat and he handed it to the waiting maid with a cautious little bow. He got a somewhat insolent (but un-noticed by the others) curtsey in return. Sukie Spooner took Maisie by the arm and commandeered her into the parlour. This left Horse alone with the truculent servant. He began to take off his coat and she looked him up and down and hissed at him: 'Look at you, Horse. All dressed up, pretending to be a gentleman. What do you think you're up to?'

'Just helping a friend, Mildred.'

The maid scowled: 'Aye - helping her off with her petticoats, like you did with me.'

'Horse grinned: The way I remember, Mildred, you didn't need no help to get those petticoats off, girl.'

'Give me that coat. Ye'd better get in to your hoity-toity pals before they work out how common you are.'

Horse handed over the coat. He put his hand on her arm and looked around at the opulent surroundings: 'I ain't changed, Mildred. You're the one what's living in a mansion now.' He looked her in the eye: 'You done wery well for yourself, my dear, wery well. You should be proud.'

Unexpectedly, tears began to well up in the servant's eyes: 'Don't be fooled by them, Horse. Don't be fooled by all that,' (here she mimicked Sukie's effusive delivery) "Greeeen'. The things I've seen in that room. They women are monsters. Liars. The two of them. And they treat people like…'

The simile was interrupted by the cooing voice of Suki Spooner from the other room, a pet rabbit with a spine of steel: 'Mil-dred - what have you done with our charming Englishman?'

The maid turned her face and walked away.

*****

For the first time since they had met, Harry Humbie appeared to be interested in the proceedings that involved him so nearly. Was that a smile? 'The wrong body? The wrong body???'

Kane frowned: 'You will forgive me for saying, sir, but you appear to be amused.'

There were three people in the consultation rooms of Abernathy and Hawkes: Edward Kane, Advocate, senior partner, John Hawkes (taking scratchy notes with his quill pen) and languid client, Harry Humbie, son of the recently deceased Alexander Humbie.

The young Humbie shook his head: 'The old man was a bit of a practical joker. I wager he would have liked this.' He took a sip from the bone china cup and looked thoughtful for a moment: 'I wonder if he planned the whole thing…'

Solicitor Hawkes shook his head: 'Oh, that would have been impossible, sir. The whole procedure around what happens to those found...' (again, he tried to be sensitive) '…in these unusual circumstances…are strictly regulated.'

'Obviously not strictly enough.' Humbie gave a lazy sigh: 'So, where is the old boy's body now?'

Hawkes looked sheepish: 'I regret to say, Mr Humbie, that we don't know, sir. I have arranged another meeting with Professor Peterson tomorrow and he will have retrieved the full notes of all the examinations from the day in question.'

Silence in the room. Then, out of nowhere, Harry Humbie spoke: 'Ha! Disappeared. The old man…he always wanted a Viking funeral. Did you know that?'

Solicitor, Hawkes, stopped his scratchy writing for a moment and looked up: 'Beg your pardon, sir?'

'My father. He always said that - for his funeral - he would like a Viking funeral - a burning ship and all that.'

The solicitor looked horrified: 'Oh Mr. Humbie, I'm not sure that the authorities would allow such a thing.'

'My family is part-Viking. 'Humbie' is a Viking name…you know that, surely?'

The lawyer shifted in his seat waiting for the next bizarre statement. Hawkes smiled and muttered: 'No sir, I was not aware…'

'My forebears hail from Jura - 'The Deer Island'. We still have a house there. A cottage. The old man used to call it 'hame'. Visited it once. Filthy little place.'

Mr Hawkes went into obsequious mode: 'Abernathy and Hawkes had the honour of being your father's firm of lawyers for more than two decades. He was certainly a man of singular energies.'

Humbie guffawed: "Singular energies'. He used to joke (and I think it was a joke) that he inherited his - and I'm not sure how to put this - his 'singular' energy - a sort of savage energy anyway - from his marauding forefathers. It was that urge to conquer every single day that woke him up at four of the clock each morning and sent him out into this unfriendly world to seize his fortune.' He raised his teacup as if in cheers: 'Carpe diem and all that.'

Hawkes gave a knowing nod: 'Carpe diem - seize the day…'

Humbie mock-scolded his solicitor: 'Wrong, Mr Hawkes. 'Carpe diem' means 'pluck the day', not seize it. 'Seize' would be 'cape diem'. A common misconception. I only know that because the distinction - the difference of that single letter - was beaten into me by an enthusiastic Latin master. The beating itself, however, was a beating of the highest quality since it was administered at one of the best boarding schools that money could buy.'

Neither Kane nor Hawkes knew how to respond to this brittle type of humour, so they both said nothing. Humbie continued: 'The old man would often remark that I lacked the Viking spirit. My response would be that it was beaten out of me so that I could become what he wanted me to be. A gentleman.' He nodded to himself: 'Anyway, I suppose that I must let you lawyers get on with my business in any way you see fit.' He picked up his top hat from the desk: 'No doubt you will keep me informed of your discussions with the good professor tomorrow. Until then,' he gave a shallow bow, 'I bid you good day.'

Chapter Nine

I Built the Pyramids

Having waded through the effusive welcome by Sukie Spooner and then a perfunctory introduction with the other Supernal Sister, medium Sarah Spooner, Mr Horse found himself sitting on a chesterfield, bone china cup and saucer in his hand, trying to look invisible. After a time, Sarah Spooner returned from her 'preparations' and bid her guests be seated at the round table.

'In a circle please, hold hands in a circle…'

Horse placed himself beside his companion Maisie Mount as the maids began to blow out the candles in the parlour. The older sister, Sarah Spooner, in commanding mode, was not to be meddled with: 'Open your minds. Open your hearts. Let the Life Force open the gateway to the Realm of the Dead.' (On this last word, her voice fell deeper and deeper into a kid of low growl). She closed her eyes and began the summoning: 'Spirits of those who have passed - make yourselves known to those who believe.' Nothing happened for a moment. But then a knocking. From somewhere. Mr Horse turned his head towards the door - was someone trying to get in? No - the knocking was more muffled. Hard to tell where it was coming from. But faster now. More insistent. Horse looked around in the gloom. The candles had been extinguished and he could only really make out the outline of the figures of those around the table. People were sitting with their eyes shut now. Everyone except the medium, Sarah Spooner. Horse looked over. Through the gloom, Horse could see the stern face of Sarah Spooner. Staring directly at him.

*****

'I did not expect to find you here so late, my friend.'

The Advocates Library was emptying in dribs and drabs now as Counsel of all vintage were receiving their hats and gloves and about to embark upon the twenty-minute walk downhill to their homes in the Edinburgh New Town.

Kane's friend and colleague, Collins, sat in the library almost hidden behind a veritable fort constructed entirely of books. Collins waved a greeting to his friend: 'Edward, my dear friend, I hope that your evening has been more interesting than mine.'

Kane thought for a moment, then: 'Perhaps a little too interesting, Collins.' He motioned to the books: 'But I'm afraid that I am disturbing you, my friend…'

Collins threw up his hands: 'Edward you are, in fact an answer to a prayer in the form of a welcome distraction. Now let's see if we can't persuade one of the Faculty servants to produce a steaming pot of coffee and you can tell me all about it…'

*****

'Yes - I am the spirit of a slave boy of ancient Egypt…'

Sarah Spooner's face was contorted into ugliness as she channelled the latest soul from the other side. Mr Horse sat at the round table holding the hands of the others on each side. He could feel the fear in the tight grasp of his companion, Maisie Mount.

The medium continued: 'Yes - I built the pyramids, like my father and my grandfather before me…'

Horse leaned over and whispered into Maisie's ear: 'Blimey - didn't know it was a family business…'

Sarah Spooner began to roll her head around. Her eyes began to flutter. At last, she came to a stop and the eyes started to bulge. She looked up at the ceiling. Then, slowly, slowly, slowly lowered her head and gave a low moan. And began to speak. In French:

'Quelqu'un est arrive…'

At this point, the other Supernal Sister - pretty Sukie Spooner - began to chirrup: 'Ooooh - we seem to have another visitor now. One who refuses to speak English.' With a coquettish tilting of the head: 'My sister's prodigious – dare I say 'heavenly' or 'supernal' - abilities have taken us all over the world and – fortunately…' (a little blush here) '…we have become proficient in a number of different tongues. This one is clearly French.' There was a murmur of disapproval around the table. Waterloo might have been a generation ago, but the bitterness lingered.

Pretty little Sukie continued: 'I shall speak to this spirit in his own tongue and find out what is troubling him.' She cleared her throat, then: 'Oh, esprit du pays des morts - qu'est-ce qui vous trouble, mon ami?'

The other Spooner sister fluttered her eyes and croaked: 'Quelqu'un est arrive…'

Sukie turned to the group at the table, translating: "Someone has come". She turned back to the spirit: 'Yes…um…Oui?'

Medium, Sarah Spooner, began to writhe in her seat as if being tortured, her speech now a gasp through tears: 'Quelqu'un est arrive…'

Sukie nodded: 'Yes - I think we got that bit.'

'Quelqu'un qui…'

'Yes?'

'Quelqu'un qui n'a aucun respect pour les dons des morts.'

Suki knotted her perfect eyebrows and turned back to the group: 'According to the spirit, we have someone here who has no respect for the…um…the 'gifts of the dead'. I shall remind this unfortunate that we are all friends here'. She turned back to the spirit: 'Mais, monsieur, nous sommes tous amis ici…'

The medium shook her head: 'Non - Je peux le voir avec tes yeux - un étranger detest…'

Suki gave a nervous little titter and turned back to the people at the table: 'I'm afraid that our friend on the other side has rather taken agin one of our party…'

'Un homme…'

'A man…'

'…avec l'âme d'un chien…'

Sukie frowned as she translated: 'A man…with the soul of a dog…'

The eyes of the medium bulged: '…mais le charactere…'

'…but the character…'

'…d'un cheval.'

Sukie concentrated and nodded as she translated: 'a man…with the soul of a dog…but the character…of a horse.'

She turned and looked at Mr Horse.

And at that point, the circular wooden table began to float. Two feet in the air.

*****

Chapter Ten

Kill or be Killed

Collins frowned. 'Well, my friend, it sounds very shoddy to me.' In the Reading Room, supplies of fresh, steaming coffee secured, Collins had listened to his friend Kane and was shaking his head as he polished his glasses with a small piece of silk.

Edward Kane nodded: 'Yes. Unfortunate. I agree, my friend.'

Collins shook his head: 'Worse than unfortunate, Edward. Worse than that. Consider the facts: a person of substance is taken ill on a coach and dies in the course of the journey.'

Kane sipped his coffee: 'Yes…'

'The body is unclaimed, so as a matter of law – after the relevant period and duly certificated - it becomes eligible to be sent to the anatomy rooms of the university.'

'Correct.'

Kane sat back in his chair. For once he felt the equal to his friend Collins in a matter of law, since Kane had spent an entire day in the Advocates Library poring over the legislation.

It had become increasingly clear that in the last twenty years there had been an explosion in the number of students studying Medicine in the universities. The students required to have a firm grasp of anatomy. In order to obtain such a firm grasp, dead bodies were required for the university anatomy tables. In previous times, grave robbing - a method of procuring and supplying such bodies - had been rife (many still recounted their memories of those two wayward Irishmen, Burke and Hare). Universities were increasingly nervous about the sources of the bodies being offered. Thus it was that legislation - The Anatomy Act of 1832 - was passed to stem the activities of the self-styled, grave-robbing 'Resurrectionists'. The Act held that certain categories of dead body - as long as they had been properly certificated, were now fair game to service the steady flow of student needs.

Collins put on his glasses: 'I take it that you have read the legislation?'

'More times than I can count, Collins.'

'And the certificates were in order?'

'The certificates? Kane frowned. His focus had been on the category of body and the removal of the criminalisation of the anatomy process. The 'certificates' - were they strictly of relevance here?

Collins took a reviving sip from his coffee: 'Isn't that what this case is about? The body of 'Mr A' has been labelled as the body of 'Mr B' and has ended up on the anatomy tables. Thus the distinguished fish magnate, Mr Alexander Humbie was unceremoniously filleted and now - most likely - languishes in a pauper's grave. While…'

Kane picked up the thought: '…while some other chap - a total stranger to the family - has been interred with all due ceremony in the Humbie family plot.'

Collins laughed: 'So - what do the certificates say?'

Kane frowned: 'They were sent off to the registrar. There were notes in the papers re-stating their content, but I confess that I paid them scant attention. The date and time appeared to accord with the narrative surrounding Humbie's death.'

'Do you have the notes there?'

Kane gave a rueful laugh: 'Of the papers I have been permitted to take out of the office, these do include various notes. They are essentially formal in nature.' He bent down, undid the little belt on his briefcase, opened, rummaged a little, then produced a slim sheaf of papers: 'These appear to be…'

Kane looked up. Collins was already holding out his hand to receive the papers. Kane handed them over. Collins placed his glasses down on to the bridge of his nose and scrutinised them. He placed them on his lap. 'Hmmmm…'

Kane raised his eyebrows: 'Everything in order?'

Collins handed them back. 'On the face of it, Edward. On the face of it. But did it not strike you as curious?'

'What?'

Collins sat back in his chair: 'That the body removal certificate was signed…by a confectioner?'

*****

Susan Spooner was wailing now and sister Sukie Spooner was struggling to keep up: 'He says that he was just a boy. A noble son of France. Killed In his prime. By a man with the character of a horse.' Sukie was almost apologetic as she translated for the people around the table. 'Does that mean anything to anyone here?'

Mr Horse sat and said nothing. Of course, the message was directed at him. 'Mr Horse' was not his birth name. It was a name bestowed upon him on the eve of the Battle of Waterloo. Bestowed by no less than the Duke of Wellington himself. But the name stuck afterwards and, in the years to follow, 'Mr Horse' became the only name by which he would ever be known.

And the voice from beyond the grave. He didn't like to admit it, but Horse recognised it. A young soldier that Horse had killed in hand-to-hand combat. Fifteen, sixteen years old perhaps? But then, this was some forty years ago. Horse himself had been little more than a child himself. Kill or be killed. And why the rebuke now, after all this time? It was war. Kill or be killed. Wasn't it?

*****

For better or for worse, things usually look different in the morning. This truth was borne out around the breakfast table of Edward Kane, Advocate. Two reasonably-sized sausages dispatched, a large piece of blackened toast in the process of being consumed and the nursing of a cup of Mr Horse's tea - tea so strong that it was in danger of inviting its consumer to step outside to settle their differences - the young Advocate gave a little groan of fullness and contentment as he pushed his chair back from the table.

Manservant, Mr Horse, on the other hand, was positively sullen today. Kane tried t break the atmosphere. He held up his teacup: 'Well, Mr Horse. Your tea-making abilities have lost none of their potency and I congratulate you on your capacity to produce a breakfast fit for nobility at a fraction of the cost.'

Horse replied. With a grunt.

Edward raised his eyebrows: 'You'll forgive me for saying, sir, but your mood may be in danger of affecting your manner.'

The manservant sighed: 'Apologies, Mr K. I was a-tossing and a-turning all the night, sir.'

Kane smiled: 'I find that surprising. I thought from your dapper mode of dress last night - and the fact that you had applied a razor blade to your usual stubble meant that you were possibly meeting a young lady?"

Horse nodded: 'It's…it's…it's nothing, sir. Just a dose of the morbs. It will pass, Mr K.' He lifted his master's plate from the table. 'What have you got on today, sir?'

Kane got up from his chair: 'Today, Mr Horse, I have a further consultation with a university professor, one Peterson - a sometime anatomist - to ascertain how he comes by his supply of bodies…'

*****

Chapter Eleven

Does That Make Me a Chef?

The academic was incandescent.

'I resent the implication, sir! Resent it deeply! How dare you!'

The solicitor Hawkes was quick in attempting to placate a furious Professor Peterson: 'I apologise for my inept form of question, professor. No-one is saying…'

Peterson was un-placated: 'Are you hard of hearing, sir? 'Saying' is one thing. We can deal with that - through my own lawyers. It is the 'implication' - that scurrilous form of rumour - blackening the name of those who are its victims. No less actionable, sir. No less actionable!'

Edward Kane - a Son of the Manse - reached into his supply of palliatives. What was it that his Minister father used to say? What was it again? Proverbs? 'A soft answer turneth away wrath…'. He gave a kindly smile:

'Professor Peterson, you are the pre-eminent practitioner of the art of anatomy in Edinburgh…'. (At last - a statement with which the agitated academic could agree) '…possibly in the whole of Scotland…' (Was that a softening, now that the beast was being petted?). 'I think that all that my instructing solicitor was trying to ascertain was that when they looked at the necessary paperwork in this case, about the release of the body, the papers seemed not to have been signed by a surgeon, nor by a physician, but by a…a confectioner…'

The professor sighed, lit his pipe, took a few puffs and shook out the match: 'Let me ask you a question, Mr Kane. Let us say that you have the toothache. When you happen to purchase your bottle of 'Lead with Opium' tincture, from whom do you buy that remedy, sir?'

Kane frowned and did not answer. This would be something better asked of his manservant. The professor turned to the solicitor, Hawkes: 'I hope that our Advocate friend is better at asking questions than answering them. What about you, sir?'

Hawkes considered this for a moment, then replied: 'Well, I required to do this recently. I sent our message boy to the ironmongers.'

'And who prepared the tincture itself?'

'I assume the ironmonger. Or his apprentice, perhaps…'

Peterson nodded and puffed on his pipe: 'Then you have your answer.'

Hawkes was entirely bamboozled by this conversation and turned to the young Advocate for help. Kane had already processed the answer and was nodding. He turned to his instructing solicitor: 'I think what Professor Peterson is trying to say is this: in these circumstances, before a body can be moved and brought to the anatomy rooms, it requires to be certificated. The Certificate requires to be signed by a 'physician' or a 'surgeon'…'

The Professor smiled and puffed on his pipe: 'Failing which?'

Kane continued: 'Failing which it can be signed by an 'apothecary'.The solicitor frowned. Still confused. Kane went on: 'If you think it through, Mr Hawkes, that ironmonger who prepares your opium tincture is not acting as an ironmonger. He acts as an apothecary – a chemist, as it were - at that point - mixing up the medicine.'

The Professor puffed away: 'Personally, I prefer my opium to be mixed by my tobacconist.'

Hawkes looked over at Kane, who nodded: 'Ironmonger, tobacconist, confectioner - especially in small towns - they would all play their part in the apothecary needs of the community.' He pointed down to the solicitor's notes: 'Thus, the curious entry on the certificate.'

Satisfied that he was no longer being slighted, the professor became positively genial: 'Not like the old days, gentlemen. When a couple of ne'er do wells might turn up at the door with a body in a cart and haggle for a good eight pounds sterling. These days, the funeratory system appears to be able to supply a decent number of bodies at a reasonable price - all legal, as long as the certificates are in order.'

Hawkes shook his head and held up his papers: 'But - in the matter of the late Alexander Humbie - something seems to have gone seriously awry here, professor.'

Peterson puffed away and nodded towards papers: 'But that is not a crime, sir. It is simply a problem with the paperwork.'

*****

Kane's manservant grinned: 'So, Mr K - when that old lady in the corner shop - the one what does a good trade in sherbet lemons - when she throws some lead and opium into a jug in the back room - then she's an apothecary?'

'It would appear so, Mr Horse.'

Horse sat and took a draw from his long clay pipe: 'Blimey.' He smiled: 'Does that mean that when I gets a piece of meat that a dog would turn his nose up at, and I make us s stew that lasts two days - does that make me a chef?'

Kane held aloft his glass of milk: 'No - Mr Horse. Given our un-curable impecuniosity, that makes you a veritable magician!' He gave a mock bow: 'And I become your mere assistant.'

Horse couldn't help it, but his face fell - recalling his recent role as 'magician's assistant' at the seance with Maisie Mount. Kane registered this: 'I apologise, Mr Horse, if my attempt at humour has vexed you in some way…'

The manservant held up his hand. 'It's not that sir. It's…'. Horse had got in late on the night of the seance and had not told his master about the contact with the dead French soldier. The event had preyed on his mind with something like dread, like the awareness of an approaching storm cloud in the distance. A dull feeling in his chest that would not shift. But it wasn't time to tell. Not yet. Held up his clay pipe: 'Sorry, Mr K. Just didn't sleep well again last night, a-tossing and a-turning. You know how it is.'

Kane smiled: 'Mr Horse, given the numerous adventures to which you have been a party, I wonder that you are able to sleep at all!'

Horse laughed and lifted his old tin mug in cheers. Took a sip from his tea, then: 'I've laid out your things, sir. You said you was in court today?'

Kane stood up and stretched: 'Indeed I am, Mr Horse. Indeed I am. In an attempt to raise the dead.'

Horse said nothing.

*****

Chapter Twelve

Cuckoo in the Coffin

Now, it was well understood that old Sheriff Meikle was - in common parlance - 'as blind as a bat'. Once the court had been convened and he was led onto the bench by his police officer, the old Sheriff would take a piece of silk from his pocket and produce a highly-polished monocle that he would affix into the orbit of his right eye. Ready for action, he would then scrutinise those appearing before him with an air of quizzical scepticism. The monocle had led to the old Sheriff acquiring the nickname 'The Cyclops'. He was also known as something of a 'singular' character.

Edward Kane, wigged and gowned, stood up and addressed the court: 'My lord, may I mention the case of the late Alexander Seaforth Humbie…'

The Cyclops adjusted his monocle, studied the figure of Learned Counsel before him, then exclaimed: 'Aha!' He turned to the police officer standing at the side of the bench and gave a loud declaration: 'Aha - we have Ler-nid Coonsul here today - Ler-nid Coonsul! I hope that you gave that chair a good dust before Ler-nid Coonsul put his Ler-nid bahooky on it!' The officer - who had already had a substantial nip of whisky that morning gave a blurry nod. The case continued as the Sheriff picked up the papers and - nose almost touching them - read through them nodding and muttering to himself as he did so. He put them down: 'So, Mr…'

'Kane, my lord, Edward Kane.'

'Aye, Mr Kane, I've read through your pleadings and can I just say - they are very impressive….'

Kane bowed: 'Thank you my lord.'

'Very impressive indeed…'

More bowing: 'I am very much obliged…'

'They state your position with pellucid clarity.'

'Thank you.'

'And your motion is refused, sir.'

The wideness of Kane's eyes at that point were the index of his surprise. The Cyclops noticed this and: 'I don't know why you're so flummoxed, Mr Kane.' He picked up the papers again: 'Your application is to open the luxurious family grave where they thought that they had buried poor Mr Humbie and see who's in the coffin, do I have you right, sir?'

'Yes, my lord.'

'But you already ken it's not Humbie in that coffin, because the fella who got put in there - put in there by mistake - the fella in the coffin will have ten toes and Humbie only has nine, is that correct?

'Perfectly correct, my lord.'

The Cyclops leaned forward over Kane: 'So - you get oot the shovels and the spades and you dig up the coffin. And you open the coffin. And then you count the toes and then what?'

Kane considered this for a moment before replying: 'And then we confirm that the body in that plot is not the body of Alexander Humbie.'

'And then what?'

'And then…'. Kane had the sudden realisation that he was now being schooled in the Art of Advocacy. And he was not proving a very good pupil. It dawned on him that the fact that the Sheriff was now asking the same question repeatedly was having the effect of drilling down to a problem with Kane's application to exhume the body. He studied his papers: 'And then it can be confirmed that, as I say, the body in that coffin is not the body of Alexander Humbie.'

The old Cyclops sat back in his chair: 'Mr Kane - a word of advice - if I require to keep asking you the same question, then may I suggest to you, sir, that giving the same answer may not be the way forward here?'

(The sheriff - the same question:) 'Imagine that I've given you the permission and you are allowed to exhume the body - then what?'

(The Advocate - essentially - and regrettably - the same answer:) 'Then we will have confirmed that the…um…body in the…um… coffin is that of…um…'

The Cyclops waved this answer away: 'Aye, aye - you'll ken that the body is not that of Alexander Humbie - I've got all that. But then what?'

Kane's supply of words seemed to have run out at this point. The old sheriff removed the monocle from the orbit of his right eye and began to tap the surface of the bench with it. 'Ye see, Mr Kane, if you're honest, you'll admit that you already ken that the body in that coffin is not that of the poor late Mr Humbie. I've read through your pleadings, sir. There seems to have been some problem with the paperwork and that place in Mr Humbie's family burial plot has obviously been taken by some random poor soul who died in similar circumstances.'

He continued to tap the monocle on the bench as if it was helping him think it through.

'And when you come to open that coffin and you count those toes, no doubt you will confirm a 'cuckoo in the nest' - or should I say: 'cuckoo in the coffin'?'

At this witticism, the police officer at the side of the bench gave an involuntary - but appreciative - snort. The old sheriff smiled: 'But here's the thing: in that you already ken that the ten-toed corpse in the coffin is the wrong man - then what is to happen to the body of that poor devil once you've dug him up? That is what you cannot tell me.'

Kane had a vacant look on his face. He looked down at his instructing agent - who looked just as clue-less. The old sheriff smiled: 'So let me make a suggestion, Mr Kane. I will refuse this motion in hoc statu and you can come back another day and make it again when you're better instructed. You would agree that that is fair?'

'Of course, my lord.'

Sheriff Meikle placed the monocle back into his eye socket: 'Then it's agreed - you will come back when you want to exhume a body that you actually think is the body of Alexander Humbie. Not one that you know is not.'

The old Sheriff smiled and stood up. Kane bowed.

'Court riiiii-se!'

*****

Chapter Thirteen

Eeny Meeny Miny Mo

The events at the séance had disturbed Horse more than he cared to admit. Not the floating table. He had seen fairground conjurers do that in darkened tents (and learned later of the hidden hooks up the sleeves hoisting up the table as the empty hands hovered over it). No, it was the message from beyond. From the French lad. The one that Horse had killed in a fair fight. A message. Now. After - what? - nearly forty years? Why now?

Horse's grandmother had always scolded that the Devil makes work for idle hands, so the cure for the brooding would always be to get to work. What was it that Mr K had said about the source of the dead bodies? Something about a funeral system? Was there not that bloke in The White Hart pub – Barry Alcott - oh, maybe six months ago and he said he was working at the undertakers during the day and then getting some extra money at another job at night - labelling the bodies that were being sent to the university. Where did he say he worked again? That little shop entrance with the red door down on The Cowgate?

*****

They hadn't won the case yet, but client, Harry Humbie, didn't seem to mind: 'Queer old coot that sheriff, eh?' He laughed: 'Didn't like your argument one bit, did he, Mr Kane?

The Advocate smiled: 'He was somewhat antic, but one can't fault his logic. If we already know- as we seem to do - that the coffin in the Humbie burial plot contains the body of a stranger, then what is the point of digging it up? The focus ought to be where your father has…' (the verb escaped Kane at this point - so Harry Humbie filled it in): "Landed', Mr Kane. Where my father has landed.' Kane nodded and acceded to the wording: 'Where you father has landed.'

At this point, the animated head of the instructing solicitor, seemed to appear and bob between the Advocate and the client: 'And that, gentlemen, will - I hope become clear when we receive Professor Peterson's inventory of the bodies. I understand that he is having a copy made as we speak, and it ought to be delivered to us this afternoon. Mr Kane, sir - are you available to consult at, say, 4.30?'

The young Advocate had recently looked at his work diary, the conspicuous feature of which was the blank page and the emptiness of the days and weeks ahead.

Kane frowned: 'I shall consult my diary, gentlemen and endeavour to accommodate you.'

Mr Horse would have been proud.

*****

Was that laughing?

Or - to be more precise - giggling?

In this room?

A room of dead bodies?

It had to be conceded that the little red door had been locked when Horse had tried the handle, but its shoogly nature meant that a little dunt of the shoulder had led to it being amenable to being opened.

A great room full of long tables. Maybe about fifteen of those. Most tables covered in long cloth. Dark. Still, in the dark, you could make out the shapes on the tables. Covered with cloth, the unmistakeable shape of human bodies.

But the giggling?

Here?

In what was essentially a mortuary of the unclaimed dead?

Horse edged his way between the tables, careful not to touch the long cloths or what they covered. At last he came to the source of the merriment. He frowned. Was it coming from under one of empty tables. He knelt down, lifted up the cloth that had reached down to the floor and - as if drawing aside the curtain of a four-poster bed - peered into the darkness. And there sat two old women. One of whom was drinking from the neck of a bottle of rum. Entirely unperturbed, one of the women turned to Horse: 'Can I help you, son?' Horse blinked in the darkness: 'I'm looking for Barry Alcott.' The other woman finished the slug from her bottle, then wiped her mouth with her sleeve:

'Barry disnae work on a Wednesday.'

Horse nodded: 'Then I'm sorry to disturb you, ladies.'

Silence for a moment, then the lady with the bottle held it out towards their unexpected visitor: 'Do you fancy a drink, son?'

*****

Mr Horse and the two lubricated ladies, nestled in a spot under a draped table in a room full of dead bodies, the location now seemed as comfortable as the interior of a Bedouin tent. It is well understood that in vino there is often veritas. As it happens, the same goes for rum. Six slugs in, the veritas flowed freely. The older lady - the possessor of the bottle - drummed her fingers against its label as she regaled Horse with her exploits with the dead: '…but they had forgot to take a look at his back teeth. and there were two golden ones in there. Foreign fella. So, I soon get them out and I takes them down to the Surgeon's Hall to get a good price. And, I'm telling you, son, some of the beautiful shoes we get - I could open up my own shop…'

Horse, now joining the ladies in their convivial hideout, laughed and waved the story away: 'I wager that you could, madam, I wager that you could.' He reached for the bottle, took it and gave it a hearty pull. Rubbed his mouth with his sleeve and grinned: 'It's some job, ennit! But I've often wondered - how do you keep track of who's who? So many bodies on so many tables.' The lady gave a sage nod: 'We put wee signs on them, where they had came from, where they had been found, the age and that. The signs keep us right. But…but….' She put her hand to stifle a laugh. At this point, the other lady - 'Violet' by name - glowered at her friend. Undaunted, the lady with the bottle pressed on: 'A few weeks ago, Violet there,' she nodded towards her friend in the gloom, 'Violet thought that the smell was getting too much, so…'.

Violet - more defensive than irate now - interrupted: 'Don't blame me - it was bowfin' in this place…'

The lady with the bottle resumed her narrative: 'Violet decided to open one of those big windows over there. And a great big gust of wind blew in. And all the signs from the bodies blew everywhere.' She laughed: 'We were all running about the room trying to catch them, like trying to catch leaves in the wind.'

Horse nodded: 'But how, my dear, did you work out afterwards which sign went on which body?' The lady took a slug from the bottle and gave a sigh: 'That was quite easy. Wi' most of them. The signs had written on them whether it was a man or a woman, where they came from and a guess at their age - ye mind, some of these bodies had just been found in the street and that.' She took another swig: 'We remembered where some of the signs went, so that was easy. For example, there was a buddy that had been hangit at the Lawn Market - so that was easy enough wi' the marks on the neck and that. And a wifie that they think had been poisoned. And a couple of weans. The problem was the last two…'

'The last two?'

The lady nodded: 'The last two bodies, I mean. It was the end of the shift and we had to get everything back in its place before the foreman got back. Except we had two bodies left. Two gentlemen. Looked the same age. Same shape. Both were to gang down to the Edinburgh University. I mind they said that one had took ill in a coach and died in Falkirk. And the other one had fell down dead in the street in Portobello.'

'So how did you tell them apart?'

'We couldn't.'

'So how did you decide which sign to put on which body?'

The lady took another slug and looked at her partner. They both started to giggle: 'Eeny-Meeny-Miny-Mo…'

*****

Chapter Fourteen

That Was a Different Lazarus

The old Cyclops frowned as he pressed his nose against the papers.

'And you are sure, Mr Kane, that the body in question is buried there?'

Back in the Sheriff Court, Edward Kane was on his feet: 'Yes, my lord. Beyond peradventure. The body of Alexander Humbie was mistaken for another deceased gentleman of very similar build and - after their visit to the Anatomy Rooms of Edinburgh University - they were buried in the wrong graves.'

'And how do you know that, Mr Kane?'

'I have it on very good authority.'

Kane did not tell the learned Sheriff that his 'very good authority' was, in fact, a Cockney manservant sitting under a table with two women sharing a bottle of rum.

Sheriff Meikle nodded: 'So where exactly is the late Mr Humbie resting now?'

Kane read from a piece of paper: 'In error, my lord, he appears to have been buried in the graveyard in St Mark's Church.'

The Cyclops held the papers close to his nose: 'And where, precisely, is that?'

'It is in Portobello, my lord.'

The Sheriff sat back: 'Sounds like a very pleasant situation, Mr Kane. So close to the sea - from which, I note, the late Mr Humbie made his fortune. Are the family certain that they require to disturb his remains? I confess that I am not yet convinced…'

The Advocate cut across the Sheriff. 'Apologies, my lord - Mr Alexander Humbie , one of the richest men in Scotland, a gentleman, is, at present, buried in a pauper's grave,'

The Cyclops nodded his concession and sighed. He took the monocle from his eye and began to tap it on the bench before him. Then, as if to himself: 'There was a certain rich man, which was clothed in purple and fine linen, and fared sumptuously every day…'

Kane picked it up immediately: 'And there was a certain beggar named Lazarus, which was laid at his gate, full of sores…'

Sheriff Meikle smiled: 'You know your Bible, Mr Kane. Very impressive.'

Kane smiled in return: 'Luke, Chapter 16. My father was a clergyman, my lord. I could possibly recite from memory a number of sermons on the subject.'

At this point, old Sheriff Meikle began to scan the galley before him: 'And who is that sir?'

Kane looked down to see the figure of John Hawkes looking up at him, like a puppy expecting a treat. He turned back to the sheriff: 'That is my instructing agent, Mr John Hawkes of the firm Abernathy and Hawkes.' The sheriff shook his head: 'No. Not him. I know him. He's always in front of me arguing in this court about some fortune or another. Good morning, Mr Hawkes.' The solicitor popped up, gave a short bow then popped down again. The sheriff nodded outwards: 'I mean him.' He pointed towards the lone figure in the gallery: 'You!' The figure looked around itself to see who was being spoken to. The sheriff barked: 'Yes, you. Stand up. What is your name, sir?'

'Um, Harry Humbie sir.'

The Cyclops sat back: 'Ah - the son and heir, I presume, of the unfortunate Alexander Humbie?'

Impeccably mannered, the son bowed: 'At your service, my lord.'

The sheriff bowed back: 'I suppose you have no idea what learned Counsel and I are talking about - 'Luke 16' and whatnot?'

'I concede that it was Greek to me, my lord.'

Sheriff Meikle smiled: 'It was a cautionary tale where a very rich man and a beggar die - and the beggar goes to Heaven and the rich man ends up in the fires of Hades.'

Harry Humbie shook his head: 'Sorry, my lord - I thought that 'Lazarus' was the chap who came back from the dead.'

The old sheriff smiled: 'That was a different 'Lazarus', Mr Humbie. The moral of the take here is that sometimes even the wealthiest people end up in places they had rather not be.' He held up the papers before him: 'Rather like your poor, late father.'

Meikle took off his monocle again and rapped it on the bench. Silence for a time, then: 'Mr Humbie - was your father a good man?'

The question took the son by surprise and he seemed to struggle for an answer: 'I…I presume so, my lord.'

The sheriff frowned: 'You presume so? You are…you were his son, sir.'

Harry Humbie gave it a moment, then: 'I was…I was rather 'packed off' to school when I was very young, my lord. I can certainly verify that my father was a man of singular energy who was successful in everything that he chose to do. He was good at what he did and became very wealthy that way…'

The Cyclops shook his head: 'And so did the chap in the bible - but look where he ended up. Your father appears to have ended up in Portobello - which I would suggest is closer to Heaven than Hades...'

*****

Chapter Fifteen

I Want to Talk About Secrets

Smack!

The slap across the face was not really the thing that hurt. It was more the unexpected nature of it. Mr Horse - the recipient of the assault - rubbed the reddening cheek: 'Still got that devil in you, Mildred. Still that devil.'

'I'm looking at the devil now. The devil incarnate. And his name is 'Horse'.'

Ladies' maid to the Supernal Sisters, Mildred Morrison, also had red cheeks - but these were cheeks crimson with anger.

Horse held up his hands and tried to calm her down: 'I only wanted to ask you about what you said the other night, about you seeing things in that room, Mildred, about them sisters being monsters...'

Mildred was still furious: 'So - I don't hear from you for...what was it two year? Then you turn up where I work all dressed up and with some floozie....'

'Mildred, my dear - you was the one what disappeared - not me...'

Mildred Morrison was implacable: '...and then - today - I get a message from the cook that there's an Englishman at the kitchen door looking for me...'

Horse shrugged: 'What you want me to do, girl? Send you a scented invitation?'

She moved to slap him again - but Horse grabbed her wrist mid-action. He lowered her arm slowly and let go: 'Blimey, I should have gone to the cop shop and borrowed a pair of handcuffs before I come here.'

The lightning had passed, but the lady's face was still stormy: 'What is it?'

'I just wanted to ask you about what happened the other night.'

'What about it?'

'That thing where that dead French bloke was talking to me through the older sister.'

The maid shrugged: 'So what? I see that kind of thing every night.'

'How did they know about the French bloke, Mildred?'

'Why are you asking me?'

Horse shook his head: 'The thing about secrets, Mildred, is this. The only time that two people can keep a secret is when one of them is dead. You catch my drift?'

'You threatening me?

'No, Mildred. You know that I would never lay a hand on a woman. My meaning is this: do them fine ladies in there know that you was once arrested for keeping a bawdy house?'

Mildred leaned in and growled: 'That was found Not Proven…'

Horse grinned: 'Yes - once you had nobbled the blokes what was using it. And I heard that included a lawyer, a two members of parliament and a parish priestMildred sighed: 'What do you want, Horse?'

Horse leaned in: 'I want to talk about secrets…'

*****

Harry Humbie smiled at the old sheriff: 'I agree, my lord. Portobello is extremely nice. In fact, we still dock a small boat there, a sort of memento of days past. But I cannot in all conscience leave my father in a pauper's grave - good man or not. I am his son. He would not approve…'

The Sheriff nodded and took out his eye-piece. More silence. More rapping of the monocle. 'Your father appears to have spared no expense in securing your education or your manners. I take it that you would concede that – whether a good man or not – your father was a good provider?'

There was a hint of a grudge, but Harry Humbie finally nodded his head. Monocle back in, the sheriff leaned forward: 'And, good man or not - you will concede that he was, at least, a good father to you. You must have memories of that?'

Harry Humbie - unaccustomed to being cross-examined - lifted his chin and appeared to be looking for the answer in the ceiling of the courtroom. Then:

'I have one memory. I think that I was six years old. At that time, we lived in a beautiful old house that had its own grounds. I loved that house. It was an ordinary day of lessons and then supper and prayers and then Nanny put me to bed. My mother had been ailing for a time and she was confined elsewhere in the house. I still remember the sound of coughing from that room. I was in bed and I lay there and I watched the stars twinkle in the sky. But then there was a shadow at the door. It was my father. He said that I needed to come with him. I was very small and still in my nightshirt, you understand. And he led me into my mother's bedroom. She was lying there, her skin as white as porcelain. And my father knelt down and looked me in the face and he said: 'Harry, your mother is with the angels now.' And he lifted me up to kiss her.'

The young man's narrative had gone on longer than expected, but nobody dared break the spell. 'And I remember when I kissed my mother's cheek, it was as cold as marble.' He stopped for a moment, lost in thought. Then: 'We had this little pond in front of the house. It wasn't really that big, but when you are six years old it looks like an ocean. And my father lifted me onto his back and took me out into the garden. He put me down beside the little pond - I remember it clearly, a little boy in his nightshirt standing in the summer air. And father produced this large piece of paper - I think it was a page ripped out of one of his many ledgers - and he folded it into this paper boat. He doused it with liquid and - just before he pushed it out onto the lake - he threw a match onto it and the whole thing went up in flames. And we stood and watched that burning ship. And my father held me in front of him as we watched it burn.' He gave a little laugh: 'Years later, I saw an illustration in a Bible that showed the seraphim angel standing guard and holding a sword before him. That put me in mind of my father, that night. Holding me in front of him as we watched the little boat drifting further and further away. Lighting up the darkness. Drifting away. Like a lost soul looking for a resting place.'

Silence. Then the old sheriff replaced his monocle. Business-like now: 'I shall grant the orders. The exhumation of Alexander Humbie first - around four of the clock in the morning - and then, afterwards, the 'resurrection' of the poor unfortunate who is buried in error the Humbie plot. Then the exchange of resting places. All done before dawn.'

Harry Humbie gave a bow: 'Thank you, my lord.'

Sheriff Meikle got up from the bench.

And only the policeman close to the old Cyclops heard him say as he passed: 'Son, remember that in your lifetime you received your good things…'

*****

Chapter Sixteen

Her Tears Were Understandable

She tried to hide it, but Sukie Spooner couldn't help looking genuinely shocked: 'Why…Mr Horse…what a…a…lovely surprise…'

Horse faked sincerity: 'You will forgive me, miss, but what happened the other night, it has changed me. I used to think that the whole spirit thing was a load of bunkum, but after I heard your sister and that dead Frenchman talking through her, well…'

Sukie began to purr. She stroked Horse's arm: 'Oh, you lovely man. You are not the first to experience my sister's extraordinary - indeed, supernal - gifts. Your return is welcome.'

To someone who did not know him, Horse would have looked positively bashful: 'Thank you, miss. I brought my Bible with me this time.' He held up a thick black leather tome: 'But I'm afraid that I ain't got much money for the collection at the end.'

What sounded like a careless laugh: 'Oh, don't worry my dear fellow. We only ask that you give what you feel you can afford.' Smile - all teeth, no eyes: 'Perhaps next time you can bring your master?'

Horse nodded: 'Oh - he'd like that, miss. He's an Advocate, don't you know. And I'm sure that he would be wery interested in your sister's gifts - what with his father - a man of the cloth - died, unexpected, like, just sitting on a chair and never got a chance to say 'Goodbye' or nothing.' Now that Horse had a heightened appreciation of Sukie's role in these matters, he watched as the lady appeared to 'clock' each piece of valuable information for possible future use: an Advocate, father a clergyman, unexpected death, no opportunity for a goodbye. All very useful. She gave a kindly smile and squeezed the manservant's arm: 'I'm sure that sister Sarah could offer your master words of comfort.'

The long case clock in the hall struck seven thirty. Sukie Spooner turned to ladies' maid who had been standing silent in the corner: 'Mildred - take our guest's coat, won't you? We are about to begin. We need to turn down the gas lamps and blow out the candles.'

She turned around and floated into the drawling room.

Horse took off his coat and handed it to the maid. He gave an exaggerated bow: 'Thank you wery much, my dear.'

Ladies maid, Mildred Morrison received the coat and said nothing.

Her face was unreadable.

*****

The tears were understandable. Given that this lady had lost her four children to the great cholera epidemic of 1832. She sat at the table of the Supernal Sisters and received the words of comfort from the spirit medium. All of the children were well and happy in a sunny land on the other side and being cared for by their great grandparents. So happy. So keen to tell their mother that all was well. So keen that they wanted to pay a visit to the land of the living and stroke their mother's hair. Gradually, a face began to emerge from the darkness. A girl…no, a boy (hard to tell in the darkness). A little voice: 'Mama…mama?' The glowing head of the child cocked to one side as if taking in the strange surroundings of this forgotten corporeal world.

It was hard not to be affected as the mother studied that little luminous face in the corner. The hot tears of sorrow ran down her cheeks. The others around the table - if they could be made out in the gloom - also wore looks of kindness and pity on their faces. All except Mr Horse.

It is well-recognised that there are many ways of ridding oneself of a troublesome spirit. Traditionally, this might involve the use of holy water, a crucifix, candles, incense, holy scrolls, holy swords, prayer books and - of course - the Bible. Reading from a Bible was, no doubt, the more accepted and usual method of dispelling the ghost. Chucking a Bible was not. Nevertheless…

'Mama….mama…' was the pitiful mew from the illuminated face. In one fluid movement, Mr Horse untangled his hands from the others around the table, grabbed the Bible on his lap, stood up and flung it at that little silvery face. It might be expected, in the circumstances, that the Holy Book would pass through the incorporeal vision before them. This was not to be. In fact, immediately after the luminous eye of the child had been struck the Good Book, the all-too-corporeal urchin was heard to exclaim: 'Ah - ya bastard…'

*****

If the digging sounded extremely loud, it was because of the wetness of the soil. In the graveyard of St Mark's Church in Portobello. At four thirty in the morning. In the pouring rain.

Harry Humbie had ordered two burly groundskeepers from his father's estate to do the digging and now their spades scrunched their way down to the likely spot. No gravestone to mark the final resting place, lust a possible location carelessly recorded on a scrap of paper folded into the Parish Register noting the occasion of the burial, a date and a letter 'X' to mark the spot.

A footman held an umbrella over the younger Humbie as he awaited confirmation of the identity of the body in the grave. A number of other servants also stood around the grave sheltering under umbrellas and holding their lanterns up high, hoping for the emergence of the simple wooden coffin. The coffin it was hoped would contain the remains of the late Alexander Humbie.

At last, a different sound. A dull thud. The sound of one of the spades hitting wood. The groundskeepers looked up at Harry Humbie. He nodded to indicate that they should continue. Careful, careful, they dug in shallow heaps around the basic wooden box and finally scraped off the earth from the top of the coffin. Then they planted their spades into the ground, stood on each side of the coffin and placed their hands under it. Hoisting the box up over their shoulders, they laid it onto the grassy earth above. The workers hoisted themselves out of the now-open grave.

It had stopped raining now. Under the light of the lanterns, the steam was rising from the grass. Harry

Humbie gave a near-imperceptible nod. One of the burly fellows walked over to a large horse-drawn cart and emerged from, the darkness - dream-like - carrying a crow-bar. Another nod. The groundskeeper began to dislodge the nails on the top of the coffin. Nails removed, as instructed, the workmen prised the top off the coffin.

*****

Chapter Seventeen

There Must Be Some Mistake

One man at the head of the coffin now and one man at the foot, they lifted the wooden top a little and took steps to the side laying the lid down to create a kind of cruciform, with only the legs and the feet exposed of the unfortunate inhabitant of the box.

Another small nod from Harry Humbie. Out of the darkness scurried a nervous little figure wearing a top hat and carrying a doctor's bag and a long stick. The family physician. Summoned at this ungodly hour - at considerable expense - to confirm (or otherwise) the identity of the individual in that grave reserved for paupers. He rested his bag on the grass at the side of the cheap wooden box before him. The doctor then took the stick and poked it into the coffin lifting up the shroud that was covering the nether part of the body. He exposed the feet. No shoes. That expensive footwear had been quickly cannibalised by one of the entrepreneurial ladies of the funeratory system. The medic reached down, rummaged in his bag, and produced a large magnifying glass. He beckoned over to him the servants who were holding up the lanterns so as to shine the lights on the feet of the body and he bent into the box and studied the toes of the left foot. Much frowning and angling the magnifying glass until he stood up again. The doctor placed the magnifying glass back into his bag and then tossed the long stick into the open grave. He looked over at Harry Humbie, closed his eyes and gave a long slow nod of the head. Humbie gave a bow in return then, with a backward jolt of his head, indicated to the groundskeepers that they should load the newly exhumed coffin onto the waiting cart. Without saying a word Harry Humbie turned on his heel, walked to his own carriage, got in and rapped his walking cane twice on the interior ceiling of the carriage and ordered it to move off.

Edward Kane and his instructing solicitor, John Hawkes, had been silent witnesses to the event. Hawkes nodded his shaggy head before he spoke, this steam of his breath visible in the air: 'Well, Mr Kane, I wager that closes the chapter here. The family physician has identified…'. But his comments were interrupted by a shout behind him: 'Hup!' Hawkes and Kane looked round and the driver of the cart carrying the freshly-exhumed coffin had lashed his reins, whipping the carthorse into action. The old Clydesdale pulled at the cart, straining to extract the wheels from the muddy ruts in the ground and Kane and Hawkes required to jump out of the way to avoid their coats being splashed by mud as the horse and cart moved past.

Hawkes pointed to his own carriage and smiled. 'Shall we?'

Kane climbed up into the carriage first and sat down. But what was that sound outside? Shovels in the wet soil? More digging? A mistake surely. The Advocate held up his hand to stop his solicitor coming up onto the carriage. He stepped down into the mud and walked over to the open grave. Ah! The two groundskeepers were indeed digging again and appeared to be filling in the open grave.

'I beg your pardon, gentlemen…'. The men stopped what they were doing and leaned on their shovels. The Advocate continued: 'I understand that the grave is to be left open - for the receipt of the other body later this morning…'

The groundskeepers looked at each other, then one took off his cap and spoke: 'No sir. Sorry. Instructions from young master Humbie. Fill it up again.'

Kane shook his head: 'There must be some mistake…'

The burly fellows looked at each other, then: 'Sorry, sir - no mistake - young master Humbie was quite particular about it. Now, if you'll excuse us…' he looked up at the sky, '…we'd like to get finished before the rain comes on again.' He replaced his cap, gave a quick doff in the direction of Kane, then wrenched the shovel out of the ground and started to dig again.

Kane got into the carriage. Hawkes looked over: 'What to do, Mr Kane?'

The young Advocate leaned forward: 'The first thing that we have of do is to catch up with your young client and ask him what the deuce is going on…'

*****

It did not take long to find the young client. An opulent carriage parked beside some basic open carts near the sandy beach in the middle of the night rather gave away the location without too much investigation.

But when Kane and Hawkes came down from their carriage, they were met with an unexpected sight: standing on the beach, the heretofore languid Harry Humbie was ordering his servants around in a near-military fashion.

Nearly five o'clock in the morning now and Kane peered through the darkness at the rag-tag assembly of people and things strewn along the beach.

One group - mostly young maids and footmen - had been placed on a bank of sand, just out of reach of the lapping water and made to huddle close together, now resembling a hastily-assembled church choir.

A long, sleek boat had been dragged across the sand into the water and had its nose pointing into the North Sea. Kane recognised it as an eight-oared 'cutter', like the ones he'd seen used in university boat races.

And there was another group of people. Of a different character. Rough men. Four of them (in their forties?) swarthy, with the look of sailors about them. Despite the freezing water, they stood there in that water, waist-deep, standing around the boat, stopping the cutter from drifting out to sea. But they were clearly attentive to Harry Humbie and waiting for a signal of some description. It was still a good hour from first light, and hard to make out anything in the gloom with any real clarity. And was that a fifth man? Sitting up in the boat?

*****

Chapter Eighteen

Like a Lost Soul

Kane and Hawkes walked over towards Humbie, their feet scrunching in the sand as they approached. The young man, hearing their arrival, turned around and peered through the gloom. When he recognised them, he offered (what Kane thought of as) a genuinely warm smile. 'Ah - gentlemen - you are just in time.' Edward Kane had already guessed what was to happen, but merely smiled and said nothing. Hawkes, on the other hand, was several steps behind (both literally and metaphorically). Humbie pointed out into the water: 'We kept the boat from my days at Brasenose. I think that my father treasured it because it was the only time in his life that he ever saw me win anything. In the boat race, I mean. Humbie laughed: 'But he could not resist reminding me that I was merely the coxswain.' He nodded towards the boat: 'Still - he bought that old cutter and had it brought to Scotland.'

It was Hawkes - still not realising what was happening - who spoke: 'Mr Humbie, sir, there seems to be a misunderstanding. The grave at |St Mark's Church, they are filling it in. The men seem to think…'

Humbie put his finger to his lips: 'Hush, Mr Hawkes. All is well. The poor unwanted devil who is in Humbie family plot - albeit in error - let him rest in peace. I will be happy to lie beside him when my time comes. You can tell the old sheriff with the monocle that I was listening. Death - that great leveller of men - will not distinguish between the rich and the poor. When my time comes, the rich man and Lazarus will lie together.' He looked up at the sky: 'I see the that the dawn is breaking. It's time, I think, gentlemen...' He walked down toward the lapping water and called to the four mariners surrounding the boat. 'You fellows there - it's time…'

With that, Kane and Hawkes watched the sailors hoist themselves up and reach into the long, narrow boat. Each man retrieved something - hard to make out precisely in the gloom what it was - a matchbox perhaps? The identity of the object was confirmed when they saw each mariner open each box, then strike a long match on the side of the boat. Kane could see the face of each mariner briefly illuminated by the striking of the match. Then, with the nod of the heads in a one-two-three synchronisation, the sailors tossed their lit matches to the interior of the boat - and it went up in flames. Kane could not hear with any great clarity from that distance, but it was clear that the boat had been been doused with some sort of white spirit or paraffin - and it burst into flames in a kind of violent, fiery 'whoomph'.

But what of that fifth man who was sitting inside the cutter? Through the flames, Kane could determine - but only just - that it was, in fact, a body that had been propped up inside the now burning boat. The body of old Alexander Humbie. Yes. A Viking funeral, just as he had always wished. And even at this distance, Kane could have sworn that old Humbie appeared to be turning gently and contentedly inside the fire, like a cat in the sunshine, as if enjoying the warmth of the fire. Kane suddenly thought of his own late father and those sermons on Luke, Chapter 16 where the rich man was consigned to the fires of Hades. What would Kane's father have made of this? Here was a rich man who appeared to be luxuriating the flames.

The four mariners swam behind the ignited vessel and were now pushing it further out into the North Sea before leaving it to drift horizon-wards of its own momentum. They began to swim back to the shore.

And what was that sound? Singing? Kane and Hawkes looked over and there was young Harry Humbie leading his servants in an odd little song. It sounded to Kane like some old bagpipe tune, but one that he had never heard before. It was an Old Norse hymn:

'Mother you have told me

Some day that I would harness

Ships with mighty oars

To sail the foreign shores…'

And the eight-oared cutter sailed on the water, drifting further and further away. Lighting up the darkness in the distance. Drifting away. Kane thought of what the young Harry Humbie had told old Sheriff Meikel: 'Drifting away. Like a lost soul looking for a resting place.'

But the thought struck Edward Kane that the lost soul was not the one out there in that burning boat. The lost soul was here. On the beach. The young man - surrounded by servants, but entirely alone - standing by himself in the darkness.

*****

Chapter Nineteen

Fathers and Sons

The manservant shook his head. 'Sorry, but I don't understand you, Mr K.'

Back in their cramped quarters in the Old Town, manservant Mr Horse appeared - on the face of it - to be rebuking his master: 'You say you felt sorry for the geezer - but that boy is swimming in money, sir. Swimming in it.'

'Money cannot buy happiness, Mr Horse.'

'No, sir - but you can rent some good times with it.'

Horse sat on his stool and puffed on his long clay pipe:

The young Advocate sat in his wing-back chair by the fire: 'And what of your own predicament, Mr Horse? Did you ever resolve the mystery of the dead French soldier?'

Horse – who had finally admitted the cause of his vexation to his master - nodded: 'It was all the maid, Mildred Morrison, Mr K.'

'But how would she know…'

The manservant gave a l cheeky grin: 'You know how it is, sir. You get friendly with a girl, then a few jars too many, then back to her house and you get friendly again…'

'I do not know 'how it is', Mr Horse, but I think I understand you…'

'We'll, me and the bold Mildred was wery friendly for a time sir - if you catch my meaning - and after we done the business…'

Kane put his head in his hands: 'Oh, Mr Horse, do we really….'

'…things come out, sir. They just come out. You can't help it. You might not mean it or it might be a secret, but when you're all snuggled up afterwards. Blimey - the things I could tell you about her, sir…'

Kane attempted to divert the subject: 'And what of her employers, the two sisters, the medium and such?'

'It was Mildred the maid, what told Sarah Spooner all about me and the French bloke that night. In fact, all the maids and such, they all get a bit of extra money if they can get little bits of gossip and such about the folks what are visiting.' He chuckled: 'Mildred said that my thing about the French bloke got her an extra two bob.'

'And are you going back, Horse?'

The manservant shook his head: 'They've shut up shop, sir. Miss Spooner, the medium, she's…what's the word…'indy…indy…'.'

'Indisposed?'

Horse laughed: 'That's the one. Of course, sir, it might have something in to do with me hitting young Albert McGinty in the face with a Bible, sir. I knew it was him as soon as I saw that ugly little mug of his. He said later that them sisters would give him ninepence for putting that white stuff on his face and jumping about in the dark.'

Kane laughed. Horse continued: 'Speaking of ninepence, sir. I was wondering - with that young Humbie fella - does he not owe you a bit of the old….' He rubbed his thumb and index finger together to indicate that money was owed.

'Tomorrow morning, Mr Horse. Apparently, an envelope of ready cash will be available to be uplifted from the offices of Abernathy and Hawkes. I have left instructions that it be given to you.'

Horse nodded. 'There's a relief, sir. That means I can show my face again at the butchers, the dairy, the bakers and settle up what's owed…'

Kane gave a little groan: 'I hardly require to be minded of our continued impecuniosity, Mr Horse…'

'Then, of course, I'll be able to clear the back rent with the landlady, the Widow Thompson…'

'Do as you must, Mr Horse, to keep our leaky boat afloat!'

Horse laughed: 'Or set the whole thing on fire - like the young Humbie bloke.' He puffed on his pipe: 'Still can't believe you felt sorry for that little foozler…'

Kane sat forward in his chair: 'The thing is, Mr Horse, that Harry Humbie could buy anything that he wanted - whether it was a fine carriage or a gold pocket watch. But he could not buy the thing that he craved - the approval of his father. That was always out of his reach.'

Horse nodded, but said nothing.

Kane continued: 'Fathers and sons, Mr Horse. Forever complicated.'

Silence. Kane sat in his wing-chair, sipping his rum and milk. Horse sat on his little stool by the fire, puffing on his long clay pipe.

The young Advocate broke the silence: 'You don't speak much about your own people, Mr Horse. Your own father - what sort of fellow was he?'

Horse rubbed his stubbly chin: 'He weren't like me, Mr Kane. He was proper rough…'

'And what was his occupation?'

'A bit of this. A bit of that. And when we ran out of money, he would do some bare-knuckle fighting in the back courts of Bethnal Green. Oh, he would never see his family go hungry, sir.'

Kane raised his eyebrows: 'Sounds like an impressive character, Mr Horse.'

The manservant laughed: 'He was impressive alright. Would do anything for his family, he would. There was one time I was attacked by the Johnson brothers - and there was five of them and my dad - not a young man - went to visit them after.'

'To deliver a stern rebuke, I assume.'

'No sir. To deliver a hammer.' Horse puffed on his pipe. 'Two of them never walked again.'

Horse was lost in happy reverie for a moment, then got up from his stool: 'Time to hit the hay, Mr K. I'll get the kettle on and we'll get you some hot water for your evening wash, sir…'

*****

Washed and ready to retire, Edward Kane - dressed now in nightshirt and nightcap - knelt beside the bed for his evening prayers. His thoughts turned to his own father, now passed.

On the day of Kane's graduation from university, the proud father had given Kane a number of gifts including a family heirloom - a gold pocket watch - and a new, leather-bound Bible. The King James Version since – in the words of Kane's father - 'The translation may not be entirely accurate, but the language itself is of surpassing beauty…'

Kane got up from his knees and went over to the little bookcase beside his bed. He took out the Bible and looked at his father's inscription:

'To my son, Edward on the day of your graduation. Matthew 3:17…'

Kane knew the passage well, but opened the book and turned to the relevant Chapter. He ran his finger over the words:

'This is my beloved Son, in whom I am well pleased.'

Kane shook his head and smiled to himself.

Oh, father. My own precious father.

And resumed his prayers.

*****

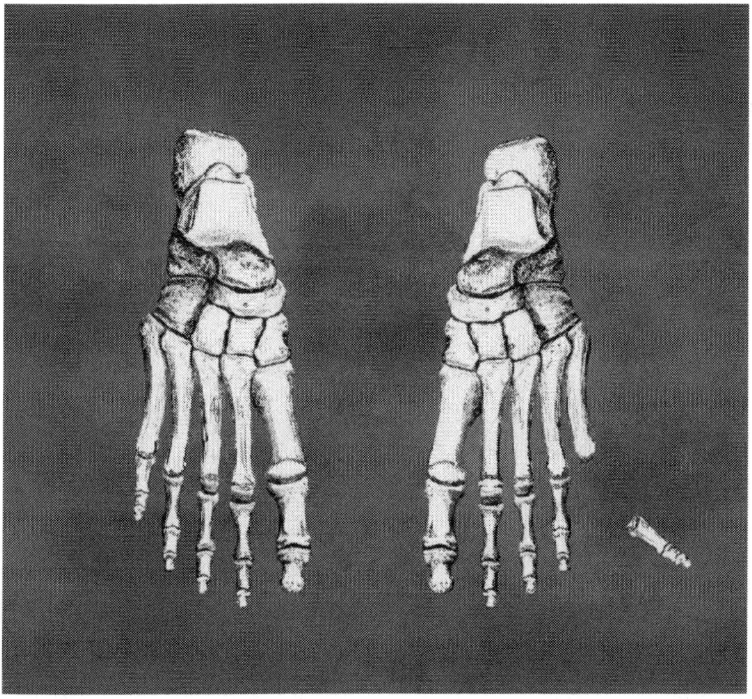

Edward Kane

and

The Hanged Man (2024)

Chapter One

A Bump in the Road

Edinburgh, Scotland 1853

No question - the hanging itself appeared to go off near-flawlessly.

The bump in the road (as it were) came later.

A decent crowd - not enormous, maybe only three or four thousand - came to witness the demise of this criminal.

But was he, in fact, a *criminal?*

Maybe that was why the people had stayed away.

Dr John ('Jack') Balloch first consulting physician in Edinburgh and sometime lecturer in Anatomy at the University - if his account on the witness stand were to be believed - the good doctor had acted as an accidental angel of mercy when he administered that fatal dose of poison to his aged father.

Fly in the ointment - the fifteen men of the jury hadn't believed a word of it. The 'accidental' part, that is. Maybe the fact that there was a concurrence of the prospect of a large inheritance - conveniently, the bulk of which was in the name of the accused – coupled with a growing pile of urgent and unpaid debts.

The day itself had been unremarkable. The gallows erected across the road from Dr Balloch's very house in the rural village of Morningside - to remind the public in general that genteel people - even doctors! - were not above The Law.

Balloch had made his way up the steps of the gallows, hugged his little brother, gave a cursory wave to some of his curious colleagues and former students down in the crowd, then offered the hangman a weary nod to indicate that he was ready. The crime was read out, the hood placed over his head, the noose applied and - as already noted - the whole thing appeared to go without a hitch.

The only noticeable difference that day was two-fold. First, the hangman - conspicuously the worse for wear and possibly still drunk from the night before - had forgotten to tie Dr Balloch's hands at the back, so when the drop came, spectators were treated to the good doctor clawing around his neck. This did not last long before the trusty noose did its work. Second, it was unusually quiet crowd. Not the usual jeering at the condemned man. It was recorded that some stones were thrown - but these appeared to be directed at the hangman, not the convict.

Afterwards, the majority of the spectators, friends, colleagues, former students (some visibly upset) left well before the customary time had elapsed and so the malefactor was cut down early and placed on a waiting cart before another doctor pronounced Dr Jack Balloch dead at the scene. Dead as a door nail.

The problem came later. In the horse-drawn cart. The remains of the hanged man were being ferried across the bumpy streets of Edinburgh. Towards the anatomy rooms of Edinburgh University for dissection. The good doctor had requested this in advance. No point wasting a perfectly good body, was there? Even if it was his own. Then the bump. A particularly big bump as the cart negotiated a large pothole in the road.

BUMP

And at that point - to the amazement of the driver - Dr Jack Balloch, recently hanged for the murder of his father, appeared to jolt awake, sat bolt upright in the cart, licked his lips, began to pull at his neck and enquired of the driver: 'Excuse me, my good man - but could I trouble you for a glass of water?'

*****

Back in the cramped - but suitably cheap - set of rooms in the unfashionable Edinburgh Old Town, it was time to acknowledge it. That distant drum in Edward Kane's head was just the warning of the massive, overpowering headache to come. The warnings were always the same. A dull beating at first as if some remote but exultant military tattoo was on its way. Then the battalions of drummers approached in formation, the intensity of the drumming unbearable, causing Kane to hold his head in both hands.

The Advocate's Cockney manservant, Mr Horse, had (at least) a partial remedy: brown paper soaked in vinegar. Applied in strips to the forehead. Sometimes it worked and sometimes it didn't. Today it didn't.

'Hold still, sir…'

Kane was clutching both sides of his head as if it were some precious, brittle, fragile giant hollow eggshell.

The young Advocate held up his hand in resistance: 'No, Mr Horse. The Battalions of Hell are too close now. I'm afraid that I shall require to lie down for the remainder of the day…'

The manservant shook his head: 'With the greatest of respect sir…shut yer pie-hole! And here! Drink this…'

Kane's attempt to reject these orders were met by a fluid move on the part of his man, which action involved grabbing Kane's nose (in truth, grabbing and *squeezing* that legal proboscis), ensuring that the young Advocate's mouth was wide open (in protest, it should be noted) and pouring a measure of foul-tasting medication down Kane's throat. The whole thing reminded Kane of being a child, when his mother required to dose him with castor oil when his motions had become irregular.

After a short, gurgly protest, Kane sat back in his chair staring at his manservant. Staring not just daggers, but a whole canteen of sharp implements. The servant continued to order the master around: 'I'm going to leave you now for five minutes, Mr K - I'll get on with the washing-up - and then we'll see if that works, eh?' Kane's face, a petulant picture, nodded (**ouch**) and acceded to his man's request.

Ten minutes later, Kane can only be described as stumbling through a waking dream as his manservant lifted the whistling kettle from fire, poured the water into the teapot, stirred the leaves and began to mash what was to to be a prodigiously strong pot of tea. Kane tapped himself on the forehead - with no adverse reaction: 'Mr Horse - that concoction appears to have done the trick…'

The manservant smiled: "Dovers Powder', sir.'

'It's certainly most efficacious, Mr Horse.'

The manservant gave a confused scowl. This was a word he did not recognise. Kane smiled: 'That is to say: the pain has gone - the concoction has worked!'

Horse smiled: 'That'll be the opium in it, sir. And I gave you a double dose.'

Edward Kane was giving this information (somewhat foggy) consideration when there was a knock on the door.

Now, some knocks are good (*e.g.* a coal-man delivering the bag of coal), and some knocks are bad (*e.g.* a landlady looking for the rent). This was a different kind of knock, as if uncertain whether or not that person knocking on the other side should be knocking at all.

Kane - fearing a 'bad' knock - whispered to his man: 'Are we expecting company, Mr Horse?'

Horse leaned in: 'I don't remember sending out no invitations…'

More knocking. More assertive now (an 'annoyed' knock?). Then a piping, wee voice from the other side of the door: 'Mr Kane? Mr Kane, the Advocate?'

Horse frowned: 'Bloomin' 'eck, sir. No idea what this is. Let me see.' He leapt up from his chair and darted to the door. Kane got up from the chair and stumbled away into his bedroom.

Horse opened the door and there stood a boy of ten years. Horse peered down at him: 'What is it, son?'

The boy was holding a letter in his hand: 'I'm looking for…'. He looked at writing on the face of the envelope '…Mr Kane, the Advocate.' The boy then looked Horse up and down: 'That'll no' be you, then…'

In that Mr Horse had not shaved that day, was standing in workman's boots, had his sleeves rolled-up, had a coarse handkerchief tied around his neck and was wearing a (literally) moth-eaten waistcoat over his shabby shirt, the child's summation of the situation was not entirely unfounded. Horse nodded towards the letter: 'Who is it from?'

The boy drew himself up to his full (in truth, not very high) height: 'Phipps and Phipps…' he narrowed his eyes, basking in his exalted position as Message Boy in the rarified scheme of the Legal World. He swirled the next word like fine wine: '*Solicitors*.'

Horse held out his hand: 'I'll take that, son. I'm Mr Kane's man.'

The lad clutched the letter to his chest: 'I'm meant to give it to the ventriloquist…' He stared at Horse: '…not the dummy.'

Horse nodded and gave the lad a kindly smile. Then smacked the boy hard on the ear. The lad staggered back. Horse snatched the letter from the messenger boy and waved him away. 'Now be off with you, you cheeky little tyke.'

The boy held an aching ear with one hand and stretched out his other: 'And what do I get for going?'

Horse leaned in: 'How about a kick up the arse?'

Offer did not meet acceptance. The boy made his way down the tenement stairs.

The manservant took the letter into the sitting-room. No Edward Kane. Horse knocked on the door of his master's bedroom: 'Mr Kane?' No answer. 'Mr Kane, sir. A letter. Looks like work, sir. Paid work..' No answer. 'Mr K?' Horse edged open the door and saw the young Advocate lying fully-clothed, stretched across the bed, fast asleep, mouth wide open with a little dribble of saliva running down the side of his face.

Horse scowled to himself: *That toothache tincture. Maybe a bit too much opium?*

Horse looked at his master. Looked at the envelope. Looked at his master. The young Advocate was snoring now. The manservant sighed. Then opened the envelope. He studied the contents of his letter, moving his lips as he read. He looked up: Cripes!

He went over to the bed and the manservant began to slap the Advocate's face: 'Mr K. Mr K. You've got to get up, sir. Wake up! This is an emergency…'

*****

Chapter Two

Three Furrowed Brows

Exactly ninety-eight minutes later, a very blurry Edward Kane (finally restored to the appearance of coherence by four cups of Mr Horse's preternaturally strong tea) was sitting in the offices of Phipps and Phipps, solicitors, confirming instructions for the emergency court hearing. At three o'clock that day.

The head no longer hurt, but it was fuzzy. He examined his notes from the consultation with the solicitors: 'So - what you are telling me is that this chap, um, Dr Jack Balloch killed his father…'

Philip Phipps, solicitor, jumped in: 'He was *accused* of killing his father.'

Kane consulted his notes: 'He was *convicted* of killing his father.'

The solicitor sat back: 'That must be conceded.'

Kane went on: 'Convicted of killing his father with fatal dose of what he thought was 'medicine'. Sentenced to death. Mounted the gallows. Duly hanged. Pronounced dead at the scene. Then, um, then…appeared to wake up in the cart - on the way to the dissection rooms.'

Phipps nodded: 'You have it in brief, Mr Kane.'

'And what do you want me to do?'

The solicitor tapped the feather pen against his lips: 'That's what we were hoping you could tell us, Mr Kane. The university carter took Dr Balloch straight back to Calton Jail because no-one seemed to know what to do with him in this situation. So they locked him up in the meantime. That's why there is the court hearing at three o'clock. To work out what to do with him. The man who appears to have come back from the dead…'

*****

'So- where is he at the moment, Mr Kane?'

Three judges. Lord Eriskay (smiling and benevolent) in the chair, Lord Lothian (ruddy faced and near-apoplectic) on his right and Lord Crumlish (like a crude waxen doll of a judge) on his left.

Lord Eriskay sat back in his chair as he quizzed the young Advocate. Kane read from his papers: 'He is currently being held on remand at the Calton Prison, my lords.'

Three judges but no single sign of sympathy for the doomed doctor. Lord Eriskay in the centre, tapping his finger on his lips. Lord Lothian on his right, still recovering from a good deal of making merry the previous evening. Lord Crumlish on his left. Not moving. Saying nothing. Eyes firmly shut. Like someone in the midst of a deep sleep.

The judge, Lothian, of beetroot complexion and clearly the worse for wear leaned forward: 'Hardly 'on remand', Mr Kane. Your client - if we can call him that - is a convicted criminal. He would be serving a sentence.'

Kane nodded. 'Except the sentence here, my lords is not a sentence of imprisonment, it is a sentence of being 'hanged until dead'. And that sentence has been carried out. Dr Balloch has served the sentence. Thus, his status of being held in prison - against his will - is more akin to remand while…' Kane faltered for a moment. 'while…'

Lord Crumlish, until this moment mimicking the dead, decided to speak from The Beyond, his lips barely moving: 'While we try to work out what to do with him, Mr Kane - that is what you are trying to say..'

Kane bowed: 'My lord Crumlish has expressed the situation with admirable brevity.'

Lord Lothian - an innumerable number of ants in his plants - shifted in his chair. 'So what is it you want us to do, sir?'

'I am petitioning the court for a judgment on his status and for his release in the meantime.'

Lord Eriskay sat back in his chair and nodded: 'Rather like our English brethren are faced with a writ of *Habeas Corpus*, I suppose'.

Kane had no real idea of what that meant, but nodded anyway, since it seemed to be getting his argument somewhere.

Again, Lord Crumlish on the end seemed to speak from the beyond: 'Restraint of the person requires to be unlawful.'

Lord Eriskay in the chair smiled down at the young Advocate: 'The learned Lord Crumlish reminds me that - in the English proceedings, the detention of the individual in question requires to be unlawful. Are you saying, Mr Kane, that in this case, the detention of Dr Balloch, a convicted murderer, is unlawful?'

Kane spoke carefully: 'I am saying, my lords, that that in all the circumstances, the current imprisonment of the doctor is, indeed, unlawful…'

Lord Lothian had heard enough and began to splutter: 'Have you no shame, sir? Have you no shame? The man of whom you speak is a blackguard. A man who killed his own father for pecuniary gain. A man sentenced to death by a jury of his peers…'

Kane weathered the storm: 'I cannot gainsay that, my lord. But Dr Balloch was sentenced to be hanged until dead. And was then hanged. And was then pronounced dead at the scene by a qualified physician. The sentence was death. He has now served that sentence. In my - most respectful - submission, he has served the sentence. Thus, the Law has no authority to detain him further.'

The judges looked at each other. Clearly, they had no idea of what to do. Kane pressed what he thought was his advantage: 'If the sentence had been, for example, ten years in prison, then there would be no justification in keeping him in prison for longer than that ten-year period. He would be released having served his sentence.'

Lothian shifted uncomfortably in his seat. Kane continued:

'In the case of Doctor John Balloch, the sentence was one of being hanged until dead. Dr Balloch was hanged. He was pronounced dead. He has served his sentence. In my respectful submission, he must now be released.

Three judicial heads nodding. But three furrowed brows.

*****

Chapter Three

The Lessons of 'Half-Hangit Maggie'

Scots Law thought that it had answered the question already: 'What happens when a 'dead' person is not actually dead?'

A hundred years before, Maggie Dickson was an unfortunate barmaid who found herself pregnant with an illegitimate baby on the way. The baby was later found dead by the banks of the River Tweed. The hapless Maggie was found guilty of murder and sentenced 'to be hanged'. Thus it was that Maggie Dickson found herself climbing the scaffold in Edinburgh's Grassmarket on 2nd September 1742. The hanging itself was pretty pedestrian except for reports that a group of medical students had started a fight when they were trying to cut down Maggie's body and sell it to the dissection rooms. The body was put in a cart. Half way on the journey to her grave in Musselburgh, the drivers popped in for a 'quick one' in a local inn, leaving the coffin in the cart. When they came out, according to some stories, they found Maggie sitting upright in the box, as right as rain. The problem became a legal one. She had already been punished in the prescribed form and could not be tried again for the same crime. So they let her go. 'Half-Hangit Maggie' lived for another 40 years. Her enduring legacy to the Law of Scotland was to change the wording of the sentence from the simple word 'hanged' to the more all-encompassing phrase 'hanged until dead'.

And that's what had happened to Dr Jack Balloch. He had been hanged. Until dead. He must have been dead, because a doctor had pronounced him dead at the scene. Unusually, perhaps, there was even a formal Certificate of Death. So what now?

*****

Edward Kane handed the paper to the Clerk of Court and the Clerk handed it up to Lord Eriskay.

Kane nodded towards the document: 'As my lords will see - a Death Certificate has been provided…'

Eriskay studied the document. He gave a wry smile: 'It appears to be in order'. He laid it on the bench before him: 'But a question, Mr Kane. If the gentleman you represent is dead, then who is paying your fee today?' He waved to the scribbling solicitors in the row behind the Advocate: 'And the fees of his law agents there?'

Edward Kane's mind was suddenly a blank piece of paper. He raised his eyebrows: 'If I might?' The judge nodded. Kane turned around and quizzed Philip Phipps, the solicitor, sitting behind him. Phipps muttered: 'The fees will be paid out of the prisoner's estate. Dr Balloch's brother is the executor.' Kane turned back and looked up: 'I understand that the fees will be met from the, um, estate of the deceased.'

Lord Eriskay had a twinkle in his eye: 'So, the fees are to be paid from the estate of a man who is dead in order to prove that that same man is alive?'

'It would, um, appear so, my lords.'

Lord Lothian had had enough: 'Balderdash, sir balderdash! A main seeking to escape punishment by declaring that he is dead while asking this court to free him from prison so that he can live out the rest of his life.' The judge sat back in his chair: 'I'll retire to bedlam!'

Kane raised his eyebrows: 'I accept, my lords, that the situation is…uncommon, but until this gentleman has a determination, he exists in limbo.'

Lothian was not assuaged: "Limbo'? He should be in 'another place' by now, sir.' The judge's ire did not extend to uttering the full word that was in his head.

Lord Eriskay got up and out of his chair and nodded to the other judges to follow him. Standing at the back wall behind the judicial benches, their backs to the public gallery, the three decision-makers attempted to hammer out some kind of answer to the legal proposition before them. Kane sat down and while he could not make out the actual wording of the dispute, he could could hear the sounds of the rumbling discontent of Lothian, the gnomic pronouncements of Crumlish and the measured tones of Eriskay - oil on the troubled waters.

After a deal of judicial wrangling, the judges resumed their seats. Lord Eriskay looked down at the young Advocate: 'Mr Kane, we are grateful for your submissions, but I am afraid that in these difficult - and, I am bound to say novel - circumstances, we are unable to reach a consensus today.'

Lothian gave an audible grunt of displeasure. Eriskay continued: 'Thus we will continue for seven days for further submission and consideration.'

Kane bowed: 'Obliged, my lords.' But this was not enough for Kane's instructing solicitor. Kane felt a sudden (and far from gentle) tug on his gown from behind. The solicitor hissed: 'Bail! Move for bail!'

Kane looked up at the judges: 'I wonder…' Kane stalled a little now, 'I wonder if I might move for bail, my lords?'

The judge in the chair shook his head: 'Come, come, Mr Kane. Bail? For a murderer? I think not. Seven days…'

And at that, the Macer cried 'Court rise!' and the three judges left their seats and poured themselves out through the back door.

Kane looked behind. Philips Phipps was frowning: 'Oh, Mr Kane - Doctor Balloch will *not* be happy with this result. Not happy at all.'

Kane had yet to meet the good doctor, but something told him that this was likely to be a difficult client.

*****

Chapter Four

He wants to see the dog…

It was getting late now, and the Faculty Servants were beginning to light the candles on their sconces in the great Parliament Hall.

'Mr Kane, Mr Kane…'

The young Advocate had retrieved his coat, hat and gloves and was walking into the great hall when he was beckoned by a familiar figure. Small, bowler-hatted, moustachioed, thick glasses - Edward Kane recognised the figure of Mackintosh of the Detective.

Kane gave a little bow: 'Mackintosh.'

The detective bowed: 'Mr Kane. I wonder if we could have a word?'

The young Advocate and the diminutive detective began to promenade up and down Parliament Hall. Soon in deep conversation.

'The thing is, sir,' Mackintosh frowned, 'I know that Dr Balloch was hanged and all….'

Kane pointed his finger to make the point: 'Hanged until dead, Macintosh, 'until dead' do not forget.'

'On the face of it, sir…' Mackintosh began to knead the knuckle of his finger into his bushy moustache. This was always a clear tell that something was not right with the detective. Kane nodded down: 'You seem troubled, Mackintosh.'

Mackintosh nodded: 'I confess, Mr Kane, that the case of Dr Balloch has troubled me.'

'How so?'

Mackintosh frowned. They walked on down that great hall for a moment before the detective continued: 'I mean, sir, the trial itself was fair. That was for the jury to decide. And, believe me, Mr Kane, they did not like the doctor one bit. Not one bit, sir.'

They walked on. Mackintosh spoke low: 'I was thinking myself that they wouldn't come back with Murder. Not with Murder. Culpable Homicide maybe.'

Mackintosh was referring to the lesser charge, like the English verdict of Manslaughter. He continued. 'I mean you get a respectable person like the doctor and he's trying to help his old father and he gives the father too much medicine and the father dies. You can see how that might be a mistake…'

'You appear to know a great deal about the case, Mackintosh.'

'I made the arrest, Mr Kane. Possibly the easiest arrest of my career. Once it was clear that the old father was dead, Dr Balloch sent to the police office at St Giles to notify the authorities. It was only later - when we found out that the doctor was up to his ears in debt…'

'Oh dear…'

'The fifteen men of the jury did not like that, sir. They did not like that one bit. Anyway…' Mackintosh sighed and shook his head. 'Must get back to work, sir. Can't stand here gossiping all day. I just thought I would say 'hello'.' He nodded towards the courtroom where Kane had just faced the three judges. 'I had a quick peek in at your case there, Mr Kane. You appear to have a mountain to climb. Especially with the good Lord Lothian.

They laughed. Kane shook his head: 'My best argument appears to be that having been sentenced to hang until dead, then the good doctor has now served his sentence.'

Mackintosh came to an abrupt stop and stared at the Advocate: 'Has he, though, Mr Kane. Has he served his sentence?' I had very brief dealings with Dr Jack Balloch. Very brief, sir. But he seemed to me to be the kind of man that you could throw from the top of the Scott Monument, but you could not trust him to fall…'

*****

'Are we out of milk? Again?'

Edward Kane, impecunious young Advocate stared into his teacup at the prodigiously strong cup of tea prepared by his Cockney manservant, Mr Horse. The liquid inside the cup was a dark shade of mahogany.

The manservant nodded towards the cup. 'That's it, Mr K. If the milk had been any older, it would have been cheese.'

The Advocate looked at the brew before him and sighed. He gave Mr Horse a rueful look: 'I suppose that it's time.'

'I suppose it is, sir.' The manservant held out his hand while Kane fumbled in his waistcoat pocket, producing a Hunter pocket watch and chain. Mr Horse took it with a nod: 'Thank you, sir.' He gave a wink: 'Usual terms, Mr K?'

Kane gave a weary nod. At times he thought that the watch spent more time in the pawnbroker's possession than it did in his pocket. He sat back in his chair and attempted a smile: 'Despite our lack of money, Mr Horse, you must be commended in providing a very good standard of cuisine, my man. That beef stew over the last two nights was more than acceptable.'

Horse looked shifty. Kane noted this and raised his eyebrows: 'Not the reaction that I was expecting to the compliment offered, Mr Horse.'

The Cockney manservant rubbed his stubbly chin: 'The thing is, Mr K…'

'Yes?'

The thing is…'

'*Yes?*'

'The meat. The meat in the stew was…it was not the best quality, sir…'

Kane shrugged: 'I did not detect…'

'It was scraps, sir.'

"Scraps'?'

'From the butchers'

The Advocate shrugged. The manservant continued: 'Scraps for the dog. I asked the butcher for scraps for the dog, sir.'

Kane knotted his brow: 'But, Mr Horse - we do not own a dog.'

'I know that. You know that. But the butcher – he don't know that, sir.' Horse gave a feeble smile: 'Sometimes, Mr K, when we've got nothing in the larder, then I goes down to the butchers and I asks for some scraps for the dog. And he gives me them and I makes a stew with them.'

Kane began to feel an odd sensation in his stomach. It was not hunger. Horse went on: 'Problem is: the old butcher is getting a bit suspicious now and he says that he wants to see the dog.'

Edward Kane put the heels of his palms into his eyes and began a slow rub. Horse smiled: 'But it will be all right now, Mr K - we got this.' He held up the Hunter and chain. 'And this will get us few bob and I'll get down to that butchers and shake a few sovereigns in front of his face and I won't need to take no dog with me.'

Kane gave a resigned nod. 'You know, Mr Horse, I do wonder what my father would have thought.' He nodded towards the gold watch in Horse's hand. 'He gave me that Hunter on the day of my graduation from university. I wonder what he would think if he saw it in the window of a pawnbroker.'

'Something will turn up, sir. What are you doing tomorrow?'

Kane got up from his wing-back chair and stretched: 'Tomorrow, my man, I am to attend at Calton Prison to consult with the good Dr Jack Balloch, convicted patricide and notorious poisoner.'

Horse grinned: 'A word of advice, Mr K. If he offers you a cup of tea, maybe say 'No'…'

*****

Chapter Five

Thieves, Embezzlers and Resurrectionists

Some people used to say that the Calton Jail was too grand for its own good.

It was not unusual, that when visitors came into Edinburgh for the first time, and looked up at the skyline, the silhouette of the prison would be mistaken for Edinburgh castle. An easy - if completely erroneous - mistake.

On any given day, a stroll in the courtyard of Scotland's biggest prison would lead to a chance encounter with any number of thieves, embezzlers, resurrectionists (the polite term for grave-robbers) and those awaiting trial.

Today, it was Edward Kane's professional responsibility to meet with a man who - legally - existed in a twilight state between Life and Death. Dr Jack Balloch. A man convicted of murdering his own father. A man sentenced to hang until dead. A man who was pronounced dead at the scene - then woke up in the cart on the way to the dissection rooms.

Kane and his instructing solicitor, Philip Phipps, a precise, nervy individual, were standing in the middle of what can only be described as an impatient mob at the front entrance of the jail. Phipps shook his pocket watch and held it to his ear to confirm that it was still working. 'That must be a good twenty-five minutes we're waiting, Mr Kane. The effrontery! Making a solicitor and an Advocate - an *Advocate* - wait with….' He waved his hand before him to show the quality (or lack thereof) of the company that they were being made to keep. Beside them, two wizened, bearded ex-sailors, scarves tied tight around their bulging necks, tattoos on their bare arms – all anchors and stars and swallows - turned around and began to stare at the unlikely and well-dressed pair of lawyers waiting in the throng. Phipps noted them, blanched, looked up at the sky and gave a nervous little cough. He attempted to change the subject: '…to wait with…with…the sky looking so much like rain.' The sailors looked up. The day was overcast and the grassy area outside the great prison doors was muddy and slushy - the result of a fortnight of intense rain.

Just then, the front door of Calton Jail creaked open and a tall, gaunt warder emerged, a large metal circle of keys in one hand and a crumpled piece of paper in the other. He looked down, squinted at the paper, looked up and bellowed: 'Phipps and Kane'. The surly solicitor lost no time in pushing through the motley throng, waving his briefcase above his head to encourage the crowd to part before him. Head down, Edward Kane followed in his wake. They got to the front. Phipps looked up the guard: 'I have my identification papers here in my briefcase, should you require…' The warder was dismissive and barked: 'Haud yer wheesht and get in the door.' Phipps held his wheesht and climbed through the prison gate.

Door safely slammed shut against the restive crowd outside, the warder walked off and Kane and Phipps stood waiting for someone to escort them to the cell of the client, Dr Jack Balloch. The solicitor gave Kane a knowing nod: 'A gentleman like yourself will not be familiar with the Calton, Mr Kane.'

The young Advocate smiled: 'On the contrary, Mr Phipps. It was here that I would consult with one Patrick Macnair'

The solicitor gave a puzzled look. Kane solved the puzzle: 'The gentlemen of the press referred to Macnair as 'The Parlour Maid Murderer'. The little solicitor raised his eyebrows and nodded, narrowing his eyes as if he was storing that information for later in case it would come in useful.

Their conversation was interrupted by the voice of another warder calling over: 'Phipps and Kane.'

The solicitor waved his hand and the warder jerked his head to indicate that they should follow. Phipps and the young Advocate made their way across the waste-ground of the prison.

Had the prison yard been a dartboard, a large crowd of prisoners had gathered around the bullseye. The warder swung his stick freely as he battered the inmates out of the way to make a path for the visitors. He shouted behind him to the guests while he walked: 'It's a madhouse here today. They're setting up the platform.'

Phipps called back: 'The platform?'

'Aye - the platform for the hanging. That's the reason for all those ne'er-do-wells at the front gate. They say they're the family. Family? Ha! Thieves and cut-throats if you ask me.'

Kane - in the slipstreams of the solicitor and warder - jostled his way through the throng and craned his neck to see what was at the centre. Above the heads, he saw a group of workmen working on a large wooden pole. The beginnings of a scaffold. His thoughts were interrupted by the jailer calling: 'Right-oh - here we are.' They entered a dim corridor. 'How long will you be needing?' The solicitor Phipps shrugged and turned to Kane. Kane reached into his waistcoat pocket to find his time-piece - but, of course, the Hunter had been taken by Mr Horse to the pawnbrokers to provide temporary financial relief. 'Um…I have read the papers. The facts are not in dispute. If you could come back in, say…thirty minutes?' The warder nodded, fumbled with the ring of keys for a moment, then turned one in the lock. The door creaked open. 'Aye - thirty minutes. I'll away and deal with that riff-raff at the gate.' He turned on his heel and walked away.

Despite the obvious creaking of the door and the arrival of the two gentlemen from the outside, there was no welcome by the prisoner. The room was dim and shabby. A bed against the wall, a ragged, brown coarse blanket rumfled on top. A table and chair in the corner under the barred window. Sitting at the table, his back to the visitors, Kane could make out the figure of a tall man. At first blush, he appeared to be playing Patience with a deck of cards. He did not turn around, but barked: 'You're late.'

It was at that point that Kane smiled to himself. He had a sudden memory of his father, a clergyman, and one of his father's favourite witticisms. He would say (with a chuckle): 'Some people are of the opinion that the existence of doctors proves the existence of God. After all, if there were no God, then who do the doctors strut around pretending to be?'

Solicitor, Phipps was nervous: 'My apologies, Dr Balloch, there was a delay in gaining entrance. A large crowd at the front gate. Apparently, today, there is to be…to be…'

'A hanging. Yes, so they say.'

A little chuckle. His back still to his visitors. 'You know, I have only ever been to one hanging. It was my own.'

*****

Chapter Six

You Have Done Evil in Doing This

The prisoner stood up turned around. He extended his hand to Kane. 'Jack Balloch. Dr Jack Balloch.' The Advocate shook hands with his new client. Balloch looked him up and down: 'You must be Kane, the Advocate, then…'

The prisoner motioned to his guests to sit down on the bed, while he drew up a chair. 'You will excuse the lack of amenities, gentlemen. I would order some tea for us but I fear that the response would involve a certain measure of cursing from the guards.'

They sat down. The condemned (in fact, now officially deceased) man engaged with a lightness of touch more suited to a drawing room than a dingy prison cell. He nodded towards the window: 'Yes - of course – the crowds outside - the hanging in the courtyard. Today. I had quite forgotten.' He produced a pipe from one pocket and a box of matches from the other. He struck the match, lit the pipe with contented puffs, shook out the match and tossed it onto the floor. 'Actually, I met the chap in question the other day. The 'condemned man', that is.' He tilted his head up towards the window: 'Met him in the courtyard there. Sought me out. Nice fellow. Sailor. Strangled his wife when he thought she was carrying on with his cousin behind his back. Big mistake, apparently. She was planning a surprise party for him. With the cousin. For when the chap returned from sea. Just got the wrong end of the stick, I suppose.' He chuckled: 'Now it's the wrong end of a rope.' The doctor puffed on his pipe and carried on, as if telling a story of friends at the New Club. 'Grabbed the unfortunate woman by the neck and snuffed her out like a candle. So, that jolly Tar asked me: 'How do you survive a hanging?' Told him 'Blowed if I know, my friend. Blowed if I know."

They sat in silence for a time. Then Phipps spoke: 'I'm afraid that they didn't allow your release, Dr Balloch. At least, not at the moment. There will be a hearing next week.'

The doctor nodded: 'I know. I received word from one of your errand boys.' He turned to Kane: 'And what is your prognosis, Mr Kane?' Balloch tapped the mouthpiece of the pipe against his chest and leaned forward: 'Will the patient live or die?' He smiled: 'You will forgive me for using medical language here.'

Edward Kane frowned: 'As a matter of law, I'm afraid that we are in uncharted territory, Dr Balloch'.

The prisoner raised his eyes to the ceiling: 'Fiddlesticks, sir - fiddlesticks. We have done our own research here. Margaret Dickson - the unfortunate barmaid who killed her child. Hanged. Survived. Pardoned. You survive the act of hanging. You are pardoned afterwards. That has been the law for - what - a century or so?'

Kane suddenly realised that he was being schooled in The Law. By a doctor.

Balloch frowned and shook his head: 'I am surprised that you did not know, Mr Kane, the case commonly referred to as 'Half-Hangit Maggie'. I should have thought that even school children would know that.'

Kane was even-tempered by nature, but could not resist: 'I am grateful to you, doctor, for your legal analysis here…'

Balloch bristled and pointed his pipe at the Advocate: 'No need to be impertinent, sir, I was merely…'

Kane cut across him: 'The case of Maggie Dickson - or 'Half-hangit Maggie' as it is known - did indeed occur, but that was some hundred years ago. And she was indeed hanged, recovered and pardoned…'

'Then my analysis was correct. No need to…'

'However,' Kane continued, 'her particular situation led to a change in the law. In Maggie Dickson's day, it was sufficient that the sentence - the 'doom' as it were – was pronounced that she should be 'hanged'. That would have been deemed an adequate statement on her sentence…'

The doctor lifted his pipe again to interrupt - Kane halted him with a raised hand: '…and so, after the Maggie Dickson case, the wording of the sentence was altered to 'hanged until dead' - to avoid…to avoid…'

Balloch sat back in his chair: 'We knew that. I knew that.' He leaned forward to make his point: 'In my case, there were two doctors at the scene.' He held up two fingers: 'Two sir. I was pronounced dead. There is a signed certificate confirming my death. What more do these blasted judges want?'

Kane thought for a moment, then: 'Two doctors? The certificate had only…'

'Enough of these questions, sir. I am not paying you good money to be impertinent…' (It struck Kane that Dr Balloch was not, in fact, paying him - or anyone else for that matter - 'good money' - it was coming out of his estate), 'Just do your job and get me out of here. Any half-wit in the street could tell you that I have served my sentence - it's your job to persuade the half-wits on the bench of that.'

The prisoner got up from his chair and walked across the room. He stared at the spread of cards on the table. He pointed down and smiled: 'You see - it's all on the cards.'

Kane and Phipps got up from the bed and went to the table. Balloch picked up a card and studied it: ''The Hanged Man', Mr Kane. The hanged man.' He smiled. 'That's me, isn't it.' Balloch held up the card for Kane to see: 'Are you aware of The Tarot, sir?'

Kane looked again - this time, he became aware that the cards these were no ordinary cards laid face-up on the table. An array of images and figures were now visible: a chariot, a wheel, a tower being struck by lightning. Kane looked up and attempted a smile: 'Ah, I see doctor. Yes. Tarot. I am aware of the cards, but I wager that I have never yet seen a full deck.' The Advocate reached down to pick up and examine one. He felt a sudden grab of his wrist. Dr Balloch was agitated, scolding the young Advocate as if he were a bad dog. 'Ah-ah! No. No, sir. Please. Mindfully. Tread carefully. We need to preserve their purity….' He lifted up a card and stared at it: '…their *power*, if you will.'

Kane had a sudden memory of his father, a clergyman, preaching against The Tarot. Against divination. Kane knotted his eyebrows. Where was the quote from again? Genesis? The prohibition against Divination. 'You have done evil in doing this…'

The doctor looked at the Advocate. 'You look troubled, sir. I don't wonder.' He put the card back down and looked at the spread on the table. 'You see before you the ancient wisdom of The Book of Thoth.' He smiled. The deck was given me by a Gypsy woman when I was a student of Medicine and I treated her child. I took no fee - being young and foolish at the time.' He stared at the cards on the table. 'But the cards…the cards have guided me…rewarded me one hundred times over.'

Balloch suddenly became lighter: 'I will perform a reading for you, Mr Kane.' He scooped the cards from the table and arranged them into a deck ready to be dealt. He held them out to Kane. 'Take them and shuffle them, sir.' The young lawyer - at some level still acutely aware of his late father's disapproval - recoiled and took a step back. The doctor guffawed: 'Your future will find you, Mr Kane - whether you hide from it or not.' He gave a sneer: 'Then I shall read it for you, Mr Kane, shall I?' Before the Advocate could formulate a polite objection, Balloch quickly shuffled the cards and laid one on the table. The card was hideous. A skeleton holding a scythe. The doctor shook his head. 'Oh dear, Mr Kane, oh dear.'

'Doctor Balloch, I did not ask you to…'

'You cannot escape the cards, Mr Kane.' He nodded down to the table. And your reading is clear.' He paused for a moment, then smiled to himself: 'Death, Mr. Kane. The card is Death.'

*****

Chapter Seven

I've left the wife and I'm hungry for love

Now, it was not unusual for people who held a certain station in life - genteel people - to run into financial difficulties. It was also not unusual for these genteel individuals to seek temporary relief by allowing certain valuable possessions to be retained by a pawnbroker for a time until the financial indisposition had passed. However, it would be unseemly for such a genteel individual to be seen in an establishment that hung those three balls outside its front door. Thus it was the job of the manservant to act as agent for the Advocate in the fine detail of the transaction. Further face-saving subterfuge was necessary. It would not be seemly for Mr Horse - the manservant of an Advocate (an Advocate!) - to be seen entering the premises of old Mr Isaacs, the pawnbroker, thus the arrangement was this: Horse would take the relevant item (always that precious Hunter pocket-watch and gold chain) to the home of Mr Isaacs' 'particular friend', Mrs Ratchett and Mrs Ratchett would approve the transaction, hand over the agreed amount in pounds, shillings and pence and issue that precious ticket to ensure the return of the watch and chain.

A smile on his face, Mr Horse whistled a tuneless tune as he made his way down to the Cowgate and the abode of Mrs Ratchett. One of those bright, sunny days when Edinburgh is the most beautiful city in the world. And one of the noisiest! An ever-increasing group of small boys, chortling and running down the street with a stick and hoop, a Newhaven buckie wife at the side of the road with her enormous wicker basket of (allegedly) fresh mussels and whelks, a coal man - his Clydesdale horse straining at the straps of the cart to the cry of 'Co-aal! Co-all!'

Horse entered into the narrow entrance of the tenement and bounded up the stairwell. He gave the door a cheery knock. 'Who is it?' - came a cautious response. Horse leaned in: 'It's Prince Albert. I've left the wife and I'm hungry for love. You up for it, Mabel?' The heavy door creaked open to reveal the face of Mrs Ratchett. A face so heavily made-up and powdered that it could have been anything from 57 to 75. She beckoned him: 'Come in you cheeky midden.'

*****

Mrs Ratchett stood in her kitchen, holding up the items for examination: 'Ye know, Horse, I've seen this watch and chain so many times now, I could draw ye a picture of them.'

Horse grinned: 'No need for a picture, Mabel - just draw me a few quid out of your cash tin, my lovely.'

'Wait here.'

'I knows the drill, Mabel.'

Mrs Ratchett got up and left the room. She walked into the hallway and produced a tiny key from the folds of her apron. She crouched down and reached into the brick wall, shoogling one of bricks before it came out of the wall. She reached into the hole - and reached in far - before pulling out a small scraped and battered green tin. She placed the tin on the floor and turned the little key into the lock.

Moments later, she re-appeared in the kitchen clutching a handful of coins: 'It's only sovereigns left, Horse. There better not be any holes in yer pocket, son.'

Sudden panic - Horse checked the condition of his pockets. He exhaled – pockets all intact.

The lady handed the manservant the coins and sat down at the table. She took a printed receipt from the top sheet of a pile of papers, picked up a pen and spoke as she wrote: 'Usual terms, then.' She placed her tongue between her teeth as she concentrated: 'One gold watch. One gold chain.' The lady looked up and smiled: 'You know, the pawnbroker Mr Isaacs has grown very, very fond of this watch and chain, Horse. Do you think that your master would ever sell them - and not just 'hock' them, I mean?'

Horse shook his head: 'Not in a month of Sundays, Mabel. Them are family hair-looms. Given to Mr Kane by his own dear father. Dead now. Wery precious to Mr Kane, they are.'

Ratchett got up and handed Horse the receipt: 'Then you'd better look after this then, eh?'

Horse studied the receipt, folded it, put it in an inside jacket pocket and patted his breast: 'No worries on that score, my dear.'

Ratchett nodded towards the jacket pocket: 'Because if you lose that receipt, Horse, then I'm telling ye - family heirloom or not - you're no' getting that watch back. I'll show you out…'

*****

Mr Horse - a gregarious individual - was wont to divide his acquaintances into two camps. Good Company and Bad Company. Problem was - especially after a few 'jars' - it was frequently the case that Bad Company proved to be good company. He was to rue this later, but for now he was walking towards The Grassmarket, sovereigns jingling in his pocket when he came across a drouthy friend, The Monkey Macpherson.

'The Monkey' - as he was known to friend and foe alike - had derived his nickname from two things: (1) his ability to scale tall tenement buildings (largely to clean the outside of windows) and (2) he looked a bit like a monkey. Macpherson was also what could be called 'a man of pairts'. Need to find a hacksaw in the middle of the night? Send for The Monkey. There's a hole in your roof and you need somebody to go up there and fix it? A job for the Monkey. You urgently require a colourful parakeet fresh in from the boats at Leith Docks? 'The Monkey' is your man.

Macpherson doffed his cap at the Horse at laughed. 'So - how's it hanging, ye scruffy sassenach?'

'By a tack, Monkey. How are you, my friend?'

The face of The Monkey fell: 'I had to call out the doctor. The doctor said I had a year to live....'

'Monkey!'

'...but I couldnae pay my bill - so he gave me another year...'

An eruption of laugher. Horse shaking his head and waving a false fist in his chum's face. Monkey wiped away the tears of mirth with the heel of his palm. He pointed at one of Horse's trouser pockets: 'That you been to Mr Isaacs' friend, then?'

'How did you know, son.'

'Spring in your step. Pockets full of siller. I thought it was 'Jinglin' Geordie' comin' up that hill.'

Horse put his finger to his lips: 'Keep the noise down, son. If folk hear you, they'll all want the money that's owed them.'

The Monkey hunched up and mimicked Horse's finger to lips. 'Then you'd have to escape, buddy - wouldn't you? To somewhere like…like…here!' He cocked his thumb to the building behind him. Horse looked up. It was The Beehive Inn. Horse grinned.

*****

Chapter Eight

Not a Dip in the Firth of Forth

The Advocates Library. The Reading Room. Armchairs and steaming coffee.

Edward Kane sighed. 'Collins, my dear friend, I confess – I am flummoxed.'

Mr Collins, Advocate, raised his cup as if in salute: 'Edward - the admission of ignorance is the first rung on the ladder of knowledge.'

Kane smiled and shook his head: 'And a shaky ladder that is…'

The friends laughed.

Collins sipped from his cup: 'I take it that you have incorporated into your studies the lessons learned from the Maggie Dickson case?'

Kane nodded: 'Not just 'Hanged', but 'Hanged until dead.'

'And the proof of that?'

'A certificate of death. Confirmed at the scene. By two doctors, no less. Once the body was cut down and bundled into the cart.'

The friends drank their coffee in silence for a time. Then Collins asked: 'Why two?'

Kane raised his eyebrows to indicate that he did not understand the question.

Collins placed his cup and saucer on the table: 'Why *two* doctors?'

Kane attempted humour: 'Having met Dr Balloch, he probably wanted a second opinion as to whether he was dead of not.'

Collins pressed on: 'Just interested. I had something similar recently.' He laughed. 'Nothing as dramatic as yours, of course. To do with a will. The husband suffered some type of fugue while swimming at the Portobello beach. A few statements from onlookers did the trick. But your chap appears to have had two doctors on hand…'

'Collins - in my case, the occurrence was a public hanging. Not a dip in the Firth of Forth.'

Collins took off his spectacles and began to polish them with a small piece of silk: 'Apologies, Edward. I did not make myself clear. All that I was trying to ask was this: if the evidence of some passers-by is sufficient to confirm death - as in my case - then why go to the trouble of having two doctors present at an event where the death of the participant is guaranteed - as here?'

Kane pursed his lips and shook his head: 'I have no idea. Perhaps they were gong to attempt resuscitation?'

'And did they?"

'Not as far as I know. But,' he raised his finger, 'later this afternoon I am consulting with the good doctor's brother, so I shall ask him.'

Collins frowned: 'Why are you consulting with your client's brother?'

Kane smiled: 'Who do you think is paying my fees?'

*****

The Monkey Macpherson rubbed his furrowed brow.

'Let me get this straight, Horse. You make out to the butcher that you've got a dug. He gives you scraps for the dug. You take the scaps back to the hoose, throw them in a pot and you make a stew for the Advocate. From the scraps.' He raised his (sixth) jug of beer: 'I thought I was desperate, my man, but that one takes the ship's biscuit.'

Horse was now (not a little) the worse for wear: 'And you can dip that biscuit in the stew, Monkey. But here's a thing. I'll go and pay that butcher now. But I thought that it would be good if I could, like, take some old mutt along with me - you know - to prove that I've actually got a dog, so that that butcher don't give me any more of his cheek.'

The Monkey nodded sagely. Alcohol has its own coherence and Macpherson now articulated the problem perfectly: 'So you need to get a dog to prove to the butcher that you've got a dog, even though you haven't got a dog.'

Horse nodded: 'You are a wery wise man, The Monkey. Wery wise.'

'You should have said so in the first place. Ma old pal, Horse - we will find you that dog! In fact…' He banged his fist on the table and the empty jugs rattled against each other, '…in fact, I have just the dog for you. I have the *perfect* dog for you. Follow me!'

Macpherson sprang from his chair and ran (unsteadily, it must be recorded) out into the street. Horse jumped up and ran out after him.

*****

Chapter Nine

The Sudden Thought of a Russian Doll

Sandy Balloch sipped from his cup. 'I'm afraid that you will have to excuse my brother, Mr Kane. Let me guess - did he insist on doing a Tarot reading for you?'

Alexander ('Sandy') Balloch - the younger brother of the not-quite-deceased Dr Jack Balloch - sat in the consulting rooms of Phipps and Phipps, Solicitors and Notaries. He offered a rueful smile. 'My brother is quite obsessed with those Tarot cards, you know. Quite obsessed.'

Edward Kane smiled and nodded. He studied the client. This brother was near-identical. Kane had the sudden thought of a Russian doll, where the identical figures became smaller and smaller the more you opened them. And the brother here - Sandy Balloch - looked identical to his brother - but smaller. Around three dolls in. Same face, same receding hairline, same mannerisms. Only one difference: a bright red strawberry birthmark on his chin. He continued: 'The jury got it wrong, of course. Finding Jack guilty, I mean. I thought that the prosecutor was awfully good, introducing the fact that Jack had accrued debts. Debts that he could only pay if the old man died and left him the money. Smart move.'

Again, Edward Kane found it striking that the discussion about the death of the old father and the possibility of murder appeared to be conducted in a relaxed fashion. He consulted his notes then looked up: 'I wonder if you could help me, Mr Balloch…'

The client cut over him: '*Doctor* Balloch. Like my brother. And our father and grandfather before us. It would appear to be a family tradition. The study of Medicine.'

Kane smiled and continued: 'I wonder - *Doctor* Balloch - if you could help me with one fact…'

'Yes?'

'It appears from my notes that two doctors attended at the gallows to pronounce your brother dead at the scene. After the hanging, I mean.'

'Yes?'

'That would seem…' Kane struggled to find the word.

The client volunteered: 'A mite excessive?' Balloch gave a casual shrug: 'We thought it prudent to have a physician on hand to confirm definitively my brother's demise, so I obtained the services of one of Jack's old students - did Jack tell you that he used to teach at the university?'

Kane shook his head.

Balloch continued: 'They worship him, you know, the Medical students. We were thinking that he could resume his post there - at the university, I mean- once you have secured his release.' He gave a little chortle: 'Which, of course, we fully expect - following your, no doubt, excellent submissions that Jack has already served his sentence in full.' The client stood up and consulted his pocket watch: 'Now, if you will excuse me, I'm afraid that I have a number of consultations…'. But his attempt to leave was marred when he hunched up and gave an involuntary little groan. He began to roll his shoulders: 'Aaaah - you will excuse me, Mr Kane. An accumulation of toxic humours has left me with an infirmity of my own. A blasted painful back.'

Kane nodded: 'I am sorry to hear that your healing vocation has left you with an ailment of your own.'

The younger Dr Balloch then did an odd thing. He clenched his fist and knocked it against his side, as if rapping on a door. It made a hollow sound: 'Fortunately, I have devised my own form of a relief - a type of girdle, as it were. I have found that it works better than, for example, an enema.'

The conversation having taken this unexpected turn, Kane did not know what to say. So said nothing.

*****

Horse was becoming exasperated: 'Look - I'm not trying to hurry you, Monkey, but I need to get to that bloomin' butcher…'

The friends had ducked into a dark stairwell in the middle of the Cowgate.

The Monkey Macpherson put his finger to his lips and shooshed his English friend: 'Button it, Horse! Button it! You need to see that 'bloomin' butcher' when you have a dog with you. The right dog. A dog fit for an Advocate.'

Macpherson walked over to a door and battered it with his fist. He shouted: 'Billy! Billy - are you in, son?'

No answer. Thud, thud, thud. 'Billy - it's me - The Monkey!'

It was at this point that Mr Horse felt a sudden and urgent announcement from his bladder - what polite individuals would describe as 'a call of nature'. He began to do what can only be described as a little dance. 'Monkey, mate, I really need…'

Macpherson nodded towards the door to the back green. 'Out there, Horse - I'll meet you out the front once I've got the dug.'

The manservant scuttled towards the back entrance, pushed open the door and immediately began to water the flowers.

Post-evacuation of some six jugs of beer, a relieved Horse made his way back through the dim entrance area out to the front of the tenement entrance and there on the street stood a beaming Monkey Macpherson. And at the Monkey's side…a dog. Not just any dog - a King Charles Spaniel! Horse grinned: 'Oh, Monkey, Monkey - you have outdid yourself this time, my son.'

Macpherson shrugged: 'What did I tell you, Horse - a dog fit for an Advocate, eh? The same breed, the *very* same breed of the dog owned by her majesty - Queen Victoria.'

Horse smiled and nodded. But something was off. About the dog. He couldn't quite put his finger on it. But something…maybe it was the six pints of beer, but…and then he saw it: 'Monkey, my friend. This dog…this dog has only got three legs.'

'It was the best I could do at short notice.'

'But we can't…'

'Oh, shut up, ye English bun. Four legs, three legs, no legs - it still needs those butcher's scraps. Come on.'

Horse - appreciative of his limited options in the matter - consigned himself to his fate on this occasion and began to study the animal more carefully: 'Well, I suppose that it's a King Charles Spaniel and all…but…'

'What is it now?'

'He's tied with a bit of string…'

'So?'

'*So*, if he was an Advocate's dog, then he wouldn't have an old bit of twine, wud he? He would have a proper collar and a proper lead, wudn't he? Made of, like, leather or what have you.'

The Monkey blew air out of his cheeks: 'Yer a hard man to please, Horse? But, I'll tell you what. Down by the butchers, my wee pal 'Manny' has got a haberdashers shop. He's got everything in that shop. We'll get a collar and lead in there.'

Horse knelt down and stroked the dog: 'Poor little fella. What happened to his leg, then?'

'Got run over by a horse and carriage. Nearly killed him.'

Horse looked up: 'And what's his name?'

''Lucky'.'

*****

Chapter Ten

What happened after that is nothing to do with me

Mackintosh of the Detective felt extremely uncomfortable. Not the fault of the surroundings. The White Hart Inn was especially welcoming and commodious at this time of day: few customers, an (over?) friendly barmaid (note to self - do not mention this aspect to *Mrs* Mackintosh); a roaring fire.

No, the surroundings were not the problem. It was the nagging anxiety. Mackintosh had placed his bowler hat on the chair at his side and was now, absent-mindedly, tapping his notebook on the table, waiting for his guest. Was 'guest' the right word? Hardly. But certainly the individual that had been invited for the 'chat' was certainly a bit out of the ordinary. Maybe that was the source of Mackintosh's apprehension. He was about to meet with George Gibney. 'Gallows Gibney' - the public hangman.

*****

'You're wasting my time, Monkey - get out of my shop!'

The concurrence of a man called 'The Monkey', a half-cut Cockney named 'Horse' and a three-legged dog called 'Lucky' had not proved a happy occurrence at the haberdashers. The owner, Manny, leaned over the counter: 'You turn up here pie-eyed - and at this time in the morning an' all - and you talk a lot of gammon and spinach! Are you gonnae buy something or not?'

Horse decided to intervene. He raised his palm to pacify the shouting shopkeeper: 'All the Monkey was trying to say, mate, was that we wanted to borrow a collar for this poor unfortunate animal here. Look at him - poor mutt - he's at death's door, he is.'

Manny looked down. Lucky the dog looked up. Smiling (yes, any dog owner will be able to tell you - dogs *can* smile). Apart from the absence of twenty five percent of his means of locomotion, the animal was the picture of health. Manny looked up again at Horse, scepticism written on his face. 'There's nothing wrong with that dog, apart from, apart from…' He gestured towards the missing limb.

Horse again - oil on those troubled haberdashery waters: 'And the Monkey here says that you have such a shop - such a shop - that we might find all sorts of collars here - fabric, leather - what have you…'

The owner leaned back in pride: 'Well, The Monkey's right about that.' He extended his arms to the goods on display: 'I've got everything here - every type of collar - leather - tartan - you name it…I had a buddy in here the other week, he was looking for one made of wood…'

Horse steepled his hands in the position of prayer: 'And all that we are asking for, mate, is for you to lend us one of them posh leather collars for - what - an hour, tops and we will return it to you afterwards.'

Manny frowned and leaned forward: 'Listen, my friend - I don't know who you are, or what part of Wales you come from…'. (Horse ignored this) '…but this is a shop - not a charity…'

Horse patted the coins in his pocket - no longer only sovereigns, but a significant amount of coinage, the change acquired from the purchase of the beer at The Beehive Inn. 'Tell you what….' Horse produced a sixpenny piece from his pocket: '…you let us have the collar on loan and I give you this. If we don't get back to you in an hour - you keep the sixpence. If we get back in the hour, then I give you the collar - and in good nick, I promise - then you give me fourpence ha'penny back. For the loan of the collar, like. Money for nothing, my friend, money for nothing.'

The shopkeeper mulled this over for a few seconds. Then held out his hand to receive the coin. He glowered – pointing to a clock on the wall: 'An hour - then that's it.'

Horse nodded towards him: 'You are a gentleman, sir.'

Manny ignored this and went into the back room to find a suitable collar.

The Monkey - who had been largely silent until now - called after him: 'And you'll throw in a nice posh lead as well, eh?'

*****

The hangman was standing up and shouting now: 'Don't you dare, Mackintosh - don't you dare!'

The White Hart Inn was more populated by this time and the patrons turned around to see what the commotion was all about.

Mackintosh of the Detective sat at the table and raised his hands in surrender: 'George! George! No-one is accusing you of anything…'

Public executioner, George Gibney shook his head: 'Ye don't fool me, Macintosh. You ask to meet me at my local pub and then you spring a thing like this on me. Well, I'm not carrying the can for this. Everything was done according to the book…'

Mackintosh frowned: 'There's a book?'

Gallows Gibney glowered: 'Stop twistin' my words, Mackintosh. Of course there isnae a book. You know what I mean.'

Mackintosh of the Detective raised his eyebrows: 'I think that I would understand you better if you were to lower your voice.' Gibney stood silent. Enraged. The detective nodded towards the chair: 'And if you were to sit down.' The hangman sat down. Mackintosh indicated the glass on the table in front of the hangman: 'And if you took a wee bit of that dram in front of you there.'

Gibney said nothing. Then lifted the tumbler and downed the rum in one go. He wiped his mouth with his sleeve. Mackintosh smiled: 'Better?' The hangman nodded. The detective leaned in: 'No-one is blaming you, George. I'm just trying to work out what happened that day, that's all.'

Gallows Gibney leaned back in his seat, folded his arms and sighed: 'I led the prisoner onto the scaffold. They read the charge. I put the hood over his head and I pulled the lever. Job done. In fact, there were two doctors there and they said 'job done' an' all. What happened after that is nothing to do with me.' He nodded to the glass tumbler on the table: 'And in case you haven't noticed – the glass is empty now…'

*****

When the time came, Horse's visit to the suspicious butcher – accompanied by the borrowed, three-legged dog - proved to be an enormous success. Haberdasher Manny had been as good as his word with the provision of the leather collar (and an opulent—looking lead thrown in for good measure) and the butcher could see for himself that the animal was real. Outstanding bill settled, at the conclusion of the visit, the butcher - so taken was he by the animal - handed Horse some wrapped newspaper containing a supply of scraps, a supply more generous than usual. The butcher smiled: 'And if you ever want to sell the dog, Mr Horse…' Horse shook his head: 'Sorry, my son. My master, Mr Kane is *wery* attached to the animal and he would never part with him. It's like a family hair-loom.'

Then a jolt. Horse had a sudden thought: *Where's my jacket? The one with the pawn ticket? The pawn ticket for Kane's gold watch…*

*****

Chapter Eleven

I can get a guinea for every drop

Gallows Gibney was on his fourth rum now: 'It was actually a very warm morning, so. I don't ken why the doctor fella was dressed for the winter and chattering his teeth so much…'

Four rums in and the narrative was flowing more freely. Mackintosh looked up from his notebook: 'I would imagine, George, that if someone was about to be hanged they would have a lot to be scared about. Maybe that was it.'

'No. No…' The hangman frowned: 'It was more like somebody acting as if they were scared.' He took a sip of his rum and smiled. 'And I should know. I've helped quite a few folk over to the other side.'

Mackintosh scribbled. The hangman smiled: 'He said he was so cold, he wasn't going to undo his collar studs…'

The detective looked up: 'Not his choice, surely…'

Gibney sat back in his chair: 'I let them dress how they like. Believe me, Mackintosh - makes no difference if he's wearing a dinner suit or a bathing suit. The rope will get you in the end.' He leaned forward: 'But I'll tell you a secret – in most cases, it's not this that kills you…' He grabbed himself around the neck and made a strangling motion. 'No. It's the drop. The drop is the thing.'

Mackintosh of the Detective was puzzled and shook his head. 'Broken neck?'

The hangman continued, conspiratorial now: 'Every time. That's what folk don't understand. That's why I can get a guinea for every drop. I have to work it out every time. The size of the man. The length of the rope. The depth of the drop. Then the drop – broken neck'. Gallows Gibney tapped his index finger against his forehead: 'I have it all worked out in here.'

The detective looked up from his notebook: 'And what if the drop doesn't do it?'

Gibney gulped his rum: 'Then the rope takes over.'

Mackintosh bit the end of his pencil. He was thinking about the next part of the conversation, and that was going to be difficult. He broached the difficult subject: 'George, I've known you a long time, and nobody doubts that you're very good at what you do…'

Gibney smirked: 'And I know you, Mackintosh, and here comes trouble…'

'…but…but - and I'm only saying what I've been told by other people - but some of them say that on that day, on the day of the hanging – that you were…you were…drunk.'

The hangman squeezed his tumbler of rum, whitening his knuckles. He glared at the detective and said nothing.

*****

The Monkey Macpherson had never seen Mr Horse so upset: 'It'll turn up, my friend. It's just a jacket. And I'm not being cheeky, buddy, but let's face it - that jacket was a bit of an old rag, eh? We'll get you another one for next to nothing, maybe go down to The Vaults.'

'Monkey - you don't understand. It's not the jacket, my friend, it's what's in the pocket.'

'And what's in the pocket?'

Horse shook his head. Speechless. He put his head in his hands.

*****

'Alright, Mackintosh - I'll be square with you.' Gibney put his hand on his heart: 'I swear - on my mother's grave - not a drop of liquor passed my lips that morning. But…yes...I was maybe a wee bit off my game that day.'

'How so?'

'The night before, that was the problem. I was at here at this table - you know, my usual table - and a bunch of young folk came in. Varsity types, with the posh voices and the scarves and the throwing their money about. I think they were celebrating something - I don't know what - and it was…'. (at this point the hangman affected a cultured accent) "Drinks on the house for our esteemed friend at the table.' And they kept them coming. And I like to be sociable...'

The detective smiled: 'So, the night before the hanging, you were - how shall we put it: 'three sheets to the wind'…'

Gibney chuckled: 'I'm telling ye, Mackintosh, by the end of the night, it was more like 'Man overboard'…'

The detective frowned and bit the end of his pencil.

*****

Chapter Twelve

I thought it was a rag

The Monkey had a soothing tone in his voice. He needed it: 'Look, Horse - we've only been to four places today - the butchers, Manny the haberdashers, Billy's hoose - where we got the dug - and where you were desperate - and the Beehive Inn. We'll have a look for the jacket as we go and we'll find it in one of thae places. But it's Manny's shop next - to get that fourpence ha'penny back. And if it's not there, then back to where we got the dug. And if it's not there, then back to The Beehive. See? Simple. Come on, then. I'd say 'get your coat', but…'

(For the record - this last attempt at humour was *not* appreciated)

*****

'…and then…and then…'.

The hangman George Gibney was well in his cups now: 'I get outside and what do you think? Eh? Some joker - probably one of those stuck-up varsity clowns - some joker has taken the hessian cloth off the top of the cart and it's pouring with rain by this time and my ropes…my ropes. Do you know how much a good rope costs?'

*****

It could not be said that Manny the haberdasher was entirely pleased to see Horse and The Monkey on time. After all, had they been a mere minute over the agreed hour, then Manny would have been able to keep the entire sixpence. But a deal was a deal, and the collar and dog lead looked none the worse for wear, so the deposit was returned. But…no jacket. Then - back to the tenement to return the counterfeit pet (and a return to the back court where Mr Horse had found relief) - but no jacket. That left The Beehive Inn, then. As the last possible place.

*****

Mackintosh tapped his notebook on his lips: 'You didn't let him hang for long.'

George Gibney sat back in his chair, nursing his tumbler of rum: 'The crowd. You get a feeling about these things, Mackintosh. They were not happy about this one. Something about the shame of it. An educated man - hanged in front of his own house and his friends. And then a couple of the younger folk got a bit rowdy and started to throw the stones – at me, would you credit it! Didn't want it to turn ugly, so took him down. That, and that infernal brother of his. The one with the bright red mark on his chin. Would you believe it - up on that scaffold - buzzing about like a wasp on jam.'

Mackintosh frowned: 'What was his part in the proceedings?'

The hangman thought for a moment. 'Don't know. 'Moral support'? Is that what they call it?' He chuckled. 'How do you give 'moral support' to a murderer, eh?'

They sat in silence for a time. Gibney finished his drink and stared into the empty glass 'Once the hood was on, the wee brother asked if he could give the older brother a hug and whisper a prayer into his ear before I pulled the lever. I let him. It was the Christian thing to do.'

'And afterwards?'

'The usual. Took the body down. The brother helped me do that so, ye ken, I gave it that extra bit of respect. There was a cart waiting so that the body could get taken up the university and get cut up. We loaded the body onto the cart and another fella jumped up on it - he was a physician of some sort - and I left them to it. They started lifting and dropping the arms and that - I've seen that at some other hangings - checking for a pulse.'

'And?'

Gibney sat back in his chair: 'What do you think yerself, Mackintosh? The doctor on the cart looked at the wee brother and shook his head. Game over. And then…and then…'

The hangman covered his mouth at this point as if to hide a laugh: '…and then the wee brother just started greetin' like a bairn. You could probably hear the howls in Stockbridge Village. I shouldnae laugh - but it was like a pantomime.'

Gibney held up his glass: 'One for the road?'

*****

'I've just come on my shift, Horse. I think it was the new girl, Evie at that time. Maybe ask her?'

Molly, the barmaid at The Beehive Inn was drying a jug as she spoke. Horse was getting increasingly agitated: 'Did she p'raps mention, my dear, that she had found a jacket.'

The barmaid pursed her lips: 'Horse, me and Evie don't really see eye to eye, so I haven't spoken to her.' She looked over and nodded towards a door at the side of the bar: 'In fact, here she is now – you can ask her yourself.'

Emerging from the storeroom was a woman in her late thirties. Her face a mask of unhappiness and resentment. Horse adopted a smile: "Evie' is it?'

The lady glowered: 'Who's asking?'

The manservant gave a little bow: 'I think you're new here. We have not had the pleasure of a formal introduction, my dear, my name is 'Horse'.'

The woman gave him a withering look: 'Stupid name. Right enough, I think I saw you in here earlier with that fella - what do they cry him - 'The Monkey".

'Yes, my dear, a trusted associate of mine. We were here earlier. And I might have left something here.'

'Nothing to do with me. Speak to the owner.'

Horse tried applying a little charm (to no effect): 'Now, lovely Evie, we don't need to bother no owner. I think I might have left my jacket here. And my little friend over there,' he nodded towards Molly, the other barmaid (who was having nothing to do with it, polishing a glass and looking the other way) 'my little friend over there said that you was working here earlier…'

The lady knotted her eyebrows: 'A jacket?'

Horse smiled and nodded.

The woman continued her process: 'A jacket? Ah. Is *that* what it was?' She gave a hollow smile: 'It was light brown and kind of raggedy?'

'I admit, it was not my best jacket, my dear - so you have seen it?'

She nodded: 'Oh aye. I remember now. Lying on the floor behind one of the chairs like an old rag.'

Horse smiled: 'Must have fallen off the back of the chair when I got up…'

The lady nodded her head as if realising something: 'So - it was a *jacket*, then. Aye - I picked it up when I was cleaning up.'

Relief flooded through Horse that the jacket - more importantly, the jacket containing the precious pawn ticket for that precious, precious gold watch - had been located. He smiled: 'So where is it, lovely Evie?'

The lady gave a mirthless little chuckle and nodded to a spot behind Horse. He looked around for a coat hook on the wall and found none. He turned back to the barmaid, a quizzical look in his face. She rolled her eyes, and this time she pointed. To the fireplace and the blazing fire behind Horse. He looked at her. Incredulous. She shrugged: 'It was lying on the floor. Messing up the place. I thought it was a rag. So, I put it in the fire...'

Chapter Thirteen

Let me tell you what the hangman told me

Collins laughed: 'I see. So, you asked the client everything - except the question that you had set out to ask him…'

Mr Collins, Advocate, had a mirthful look in his eye. Edward Kane smiled: 'Correct. I meant to ask in more detail why there required to be two doctors on the scene - but I suppose that one of them was the unfortunate man's brother, so he doesn't actually count.'

Collins took off his tortoiseshell glasses and he began to nibble the end of one of the arms: 'Or to provide double proof that the hanged man was dead?'

Kane laughed: "Hanged by the neck until *doubly* dead'…'

Collins nodded: 'That would certainly be proof well beyond the balance of probabilities.'

Edward Kane frowned: 'But for what reason?'

'That - Edward - is what I suspect you will find out when you are interrogated by our three judges.'

The conversation was interrupted by the silent attendance of a Faculty Servant, standing at the side of the table. Kane looked up and smiled, inviting conversation. The Servant gave a little bow: 'I apologise for the interruption, Mr Kane, but there is a gentleman in the Hall asking to speak to you.'

'Did he give his name?'

'That would be a Mr Mackintosh. A detective. He says that you will know what it concerns…'

*****

'There's something afoot here, Mr Kane. I can smell it…'

Mackintosh of the Detective and Edward Kane were walking up and down the great Parliament Hall, the detective rubbing his bushy moustache with the knuckle of his index finger.

Kane raised his eyebrows: 'Mackintosh, you will appreciate that. I cannot comment on this. All communications between client and Counsel are entirely confidential. He could tell me at consultation that he killed a hundred fathers, but that would remain between him and me…'

'I appreciate that sir, I do. But here's the thing: the man who was hanged is not your client. He is dead - or so he claims.'

'Still, I…um…'

Mackintosh nodded: 'We can make this simple, sir: who is paying your bill?'

The young Advocate frowned: 'The money will come from…from his estate, I suppose.'

'Which proves that he is dead, then, doesn't it. I should think that your client is actually the dead man's brother - as executor?'

The conversation had now assumed all the character of a university examination question. And a hard one at that. Kane stopped in his tracks: 'Mackintosh, please excuse me. I do not mean to appear rude, but you were the one who has asked to speak to me. Within the limits of my own responsibilities, how can I help you, sir?'

Mackintosh frowned: 'I know that you're an honest man, Mr Kane, and I know that you would never - knowingly - partake in fraud. But this whole case…'

Kane held up his hand to stay the conversation: 'Forgive me, sir - but what I will not partake in is idle gossip. This whole situation is difficult enough, without…'

'Let me tell you what the hangman told me. Then you can decide for yourself.'

The Advocate and the detective walked up and down the length of Parliament Hall.

*****

CLUNK - the jug of beer was set down abruptly onto the table before Mr Horse. He looked up at barmaid Molly: 'Molly, my dear, I didn't order…'

The barmaid smiled: 'Shut yer pie-hole and drink up. I'm fed up looking at that miserable face of yours staring into the fire there. What's the matter with you? You look like a man that lost a shilling and found a farthing.'

Horse stared into the flames. He placed his hand around the jug: 'I lost more than that, my lovely. A lot more than that.'

Molly rolled her eyes: 'A jacket? Is that it? A jacket? You're acting like you lost your mother…'

Horse shook his head: 'It was what was in the jacket, Molly. Something I can't replace.'

The barmaid looked at the manservant and then looked at the flames. She nodded towards a metal poker at the hearth: 'Did you dig through the ashes with the poker?'

The disconsolate manservant nodded: 'First thing I did. Dug through the whole fire straight away. Found nothing but ashes.'

Molly gave a smile. 'Funny, that, eh?' A casual observer might have detected an odd, almost knowing quality to that smile, but Horse was too grief-stricken to notice. She shook her head. 'Drink up, Horse, drink up'

*****

Later that evening, Edward Kane sat back in his wing chair by the fire. 'Ahhh, Mr Horse - that gammon was beyond delicious. I take it that the butcher was more than pleased to have his bill finally settled.'

Horse gave a grunt of assent. Kane detected a measure of dissatisfaction in the sound and attempted to cheer his man up: 'I hear from Mr Phipps, the solicitor, that payment for the case of Dr Balloch will be with us very soon, so we can rescue our watch ere long….'

Horse said nothing.

Kane smiled: 'So - all being well - no canine 'scraps' for a while, eh?'

Horse. Nothing.

The Advocate pressed on: 'Are you feeling quite well, Mr Horse. You hardly touched that excellent meal. And - if you don't mind me saying so - you appear devoid of your usual ebullience.'

Mr Horse - who was yet to confess the destruction of the pawn ticket and the concomitant loss of the gold watch - was removing the dirty dishes from the table: 'If I knew what you was talking about, Mr K, I might agree.' He sighed: 'Been a long day. If it's all one, sir, I'll get these dishes done - then hit the hay.'

*****

Chapter Fourteen

Lovely evening for a stroll, ennit?

The Following Day

Mr Horse had been standing outside the Beehive Inn now for twenty minutes. Having been inside to try to catch Molly, the barmaid, he had encountered a less-than-friendly greeting - 'Oh - it's you again' - by her truculent colleague, Evie. One of the regulars had pointed to the clock on the wall and remarked that Molly usually started at four o'clock, and it was just after three now.

Horse decided to have a wander in the Grassmarket while he waited. He stopped at the West Bow and gave a little smile to himself. Wasn't it over here where they used to keep 'The Maiden'? The old gallows for the public executions. That's what the older folks said, anyway. Right here in the middle of the West Bow. An old fashioned gallows, it was. They would put your head through the wooden hole, then a great big sharp blade would come down and chop it off. And all in public. Wonder why they changed it to hanging? If they'd kept The Maiden going, then you wouldn't have the likes of that Dr Balloch sitting up in the cart afterwards, would you! Horse had a sudden thought that made him chuckle: a vision of Dr Balloch holding his severed head under his arm - with the mouth saying: 'Excuse me, could I have a drink of water?'

But who was that making their way through the crowds? Horse shouted: 'Molly! Molly!' The barmaid, friendly as ever, walked up and beamed at the manservant:

'Horse - if it's a drink you want, you'll have to come into the pub, my friend.'

'It's not that, my girl, it's what you said the other night - or didn't say.' The barmaid narrowed her eyes, puzzled. Horse continued: 'When I said that I found nothing and I was raking through them ashes in the fireplace, you had a queer look on your face, my girl. What was that about?'

Molly blushed. Hesitant now. 'Horse - the last thing I am is a tattle-tale. Believe me - the things I could tell you that I see in that place…'

The manservant frowned and cocked his head: 'Spit it out, doll.'

'When you said you found *nothing* in the fire…'

'Yes?'

'Is that right?'

Horse frowned: 'You're talking riddles now, Molly.'

'You found nothing? Nothing at all?'

The manservant frowned, thought about it, puffed out his cheeks, then blew out the air: 'Just ashes, girl. Nothing but ashes…'

'Not even buttons?'

'Buttons?'

Molly spoke to Horse as if he was stupid: 'Buttons from the jacket. The jacket that Evie said had been put in the fire.'

Mr Horse stood there saying nothing, but a gradual understanding of what was being said began to creep over him. Molly sighed: 'I don't like that girl. Nobody does. We call her 'Evie, the Thieve-y'

Horse closed his eyes and began to shake his head. The barmaid put her hand on his arm: 'You're not the first one to be fooled, Horse. and you won't be the last.' She stood back. 'I'd better get to work and let 'Thievy Evie' away.' She began to walk away: 'Have it out with her, Horse - but a word of warning. Her husband is just out of the jail. And he's very big. And he is not what you might call 'friendly'...'

*****

It was not quite dark yet when barmaid Evie and (a very large man that Horse assumed was) her husband left the common entrance to the tenement where they lived. Horse was stood on the corner, leaning on a lamp post and smoking his long clay pipe.

'Lovely evening for a stroll, ennit?'

The man of the couple gave a sort of grunt of acknowledgement. Otherwise, the pair walked on, passing Horse without comment. Horse left it for a moment, then called out after them: 'A bit of a nip in the air tonight. Had to put on me coat.' He nodded over: Lucky you got that nice warm jacket, eh?'

The couple came to a dead halt first. Then Horse noted that Evie was trying to pull her husband on. Horse heard her say: 'Come on, Adam. Ignore him. He's just a drunk.'

Horse gave a loud laugh: "Adam' - did you just call your old man, 'Adam', Evie? This is priceless, this is. 'Adam' and 'Evie'. As we used to say in Bethnal Green: 'Would you Adam and Eve it?'.' Horse guffawed.

Evie's husband turned on a sixpence and walked right back, now in Horse's face. 'Is there a problem here, buddy?'

Horse took a step back, as if to admire the clothes of the man in front of him: 'That is one wery useful jacket, you got there, my son. Where did you get it? The Vaults?'

The husband was somewhat puzzled by Horse's approach and gave a sharp glance to wife, Evie. Horse looked over at the barmaid: 'Or maybe somebody found it at work and shouldn't have kept it, eh, Evie my dear?'

Evie looked at the floor: 'I don't know what he's talking about.' She motioned: 'Come on, Adam.'

'You see, my friend'. Horse pointed to the jacket, 'this here jacket is mine and your missus has - no doubt - lifted it by mistake and she's took it home for you.' Horse looked the husband up and down: 'But a little bit snug for ya, don't you think? A big fella like you. Why don't you just take it off - give it back to me and we'll say no more about it? How's that?'

The large husband smiled and - for a moment - it looked as if he was going to take off the jacket. But instead, he was reaching into his back pocket. And produced a large knife. He pushed Horse against the lamp post: 'This is the knife that I use for peeling the potatoes. It just got me five year in the jail. Because it wisnae potatoes I peeled - you ken what I'm saying to you?'

Horse held up both hands and the husband backed off: 'We have more in common than you think, my friend.' Horse reached into his coat and produced a nine-inch iron bar (affectionately known as Horse's 'Aunty Betty'). 'We both like potatoes,' He wielded his Aunty Betty, 'but I like them good and mashed. How does that work for you? Want a taste?'

*****

Chapter Fifteen

Not the usual unsettled dreams

Edward Kane looked up from his book. 'Is that you, Mr Horse?'

A voice from the hall called back: 'I'm just taking off me coat…and me jacket, sir.'

Kane went back to his Dickens: 'I thought you said that you had business to attend to.'

Horse came into the sitting room, holding up a piece of paper: 'Business sorted, Mr K.' He went to the mantelpiece. 'Now - if you don't mind, sir, I'll put this here pawn ticket under the mantel clock here - just so that we know where it is.'

The young Advocate nodded: 'Very wise, Mr Horse. Very wise. We must keep it safe.'

The manservant exhaled. Edward Kane put the bookmark in his book and closed it. 'I've been meaning to say, Mr Horse - you have been very out of sorts these last few days. I thought that I should just enquire…'

'All is well now, Mr K. All is well. I'll just get the kettle on and make us a brew.'

He paused for a moment, then: 'And then I'll tell you the whole story, sir.'

*****

Kane leaned forward in his chair: 'So - this chap - 'Adam' - it transpired that he was wearing your jacket?'

'He was indeed, Mr K.'

'And how did you get it from him?'

'We had…we had, what you could call 'a conversation'…'

'About what?'

'About potatoes, sir.'

"Potatoes'???'

'It's a long story, Mr K.'

Now that the missing ticket had been recovered, restored to its rightful owner and placed beneath the marble mantle clock, Horse felt able to laugh at himself (just a little bit, mind) and the entire scenario that had led to that whole goose chase in the first place - three-legged animal and all.

The telling of the story was punctuated by the horrified laughter of the young Advocate, who required to cover his mouth at various points of the narrative to contain himself. Kane smiled: 'Well, I suppose that she was not the first 'Eve' to take something that did not belong to her.'

'Wish I'd said that, sir.'

Kane wiped the tears of laughter from his eyes with the heels of his palms. 'Oh, Mr Horse - what a merry dance indeed - and all over a dog that did not exist in the first place.' He began to chortle again. Horse found himself laughing too: 'Still, Mr K, I'm telling yer, the scraps the butcher gave this week was wery, wery good…'

'What happened to them?'

'The Monkey took them to see if he could make the stew.'

More laughter.

Horse got up. 'I'll make us another cuppa, sir, and you can tell us what's happening in your latest case…'

'My *only* case…'

'The one with the doctor what got hanged and woke up in the cart - oh, Mr K, I don't know why, but if does make me laugh. I'll get the kettle on again.'

*****

No laughter this time. Horse sat, brows furrowed in concentration as his master went into the detail of the case. And then the further information that had been imparted by Mackintosh of the Detective during that promenade up and down Parliament Hall.

At the conclusion of the account, Horse sat back in his chair, tin mug on his lap. 'Fishy, Mr K. Definitely fishy. The more you tell me about them two doctor brothers…I don't know. The more you talk about them, the more that them two Balloch brothers sound well dodgy. The whole thing sounds like a trick, if you ask me. A trick.'

Kane drew himself up: 'Mr Horse - The Ballochs are educated and well-respected physicians, not fairground magicians barking at passers-by for the odd tuppence'.

The manservant shook his head: 'I wouldn't trust them with my dog, sir.'

He added: 'If we had one…'

*****

A restless night for Horse.

Not the usual unsettled dreams: not the fields of Waterloo, the mud, the pitiful whinnying of the horses trapped among the flying cannonballs, not the screaming, the constant threat of death.

Different, the dreams tonight. A lost dog (number of limbs unspecified), Horse standing there in Manny's haberdashery, a hook on the ceiling, a dog lead swaying gently in the breeze (breeze? It's the interior of a shop!), Manny standing there, smiling, arms spread - 'Believe me - I have everything you want…'

Horse opened his eyes and lay there staring into the darkness for a long time. He got up and sat on the edge of his little bunk. After much blinking and scratching to rouse himself, the manservant got up and made his way into the sitting room. The mantelpiece marble clock told 5.30. Not due up for another hour or so, but today was going for be different. Edward Kane was expected in court at 10, but before then….

Horse went over to the fireplace, knelt down and put a match to the paper and wood stacked there. He went into the little kitchen area and filled a large pot with water. He placed the pot over the emerging fire then went to the door of his master's bedroom.

There was Edward Kane lying asleep, a copy of 'Bleak House' lying open on his chest. Horse smiled. The candle must have burned itself out.

The manservant knelt down beside the bed and whispered in his master's ear: 'Mr K. Mr K, sir - time to get up.' Kane open his eyes sharply and realised that he had a book on his chest: 'Mr Horse, I'm sorry...sorry...I must have…what time. Is it?'

'Just after half past five, sir.'

Kane gave a little cough: 'Then, um…' (He knew it was too early to rise but he was still too foggy to articulate it). Horse anticipated the objection: 'I knows that you're in court today, sir and that you're meeting them Balloch brothers beforehand at the Calton.'

Kane blinked and nodded and Horse continued: 'But you and me, sir, we got to go somewhere first.'

'Where?'

'The haberdashers, sir.'

*****

Chapter Sixteen

Professional Difficulties

The early morning consultation in anticipation of the court hearing had become more than a little heated.

'This is outrageous!'

Dr Jack Balloch was pointing into the face of his Advocate, Edward Kane: 'It beyond outrageous - it is disgraceful. I'll have your guts for garters, Kane.'

The younger brother - Sandy Balloch, who, sitting there, resembled the older brother, but shrunk in the wash – had a quizzical look: 'Oh, Mr Kane, Mr Kane - what precisely are these 'professional difficulties' that you say are causing you to withdraw from acting. On the very day of the crucial court hearing, I might add. The crucial hearing that will set my brother free.'

Since the visit to the haberdashers that morning and then in the carriage with Phipps the solicitor to the Calton Jail to see the client, Edward Kane had tried to formulate a wording that would allow him to withdraw from acting without showing his hand. What he now knew. But this attempt at withdrawal was becoming impossible given the onslaught by the condemned man and his (admittedly, more even-tempered) brother.

The older brother was shouting: 'You will never work again, sir. I will see to that. We shall lodge a formal complaint against you, Kane. A complaint to The Dean of

Faculty himself. That will show you! And don't think that I won't. He happens to be a personal friend.'

(The young Advocate had the sudden thought that if The Dean was such a 'personal friend', then why was he not instructed to argue the case himself?)

Attempting to quieten the doctor, the younger brother became the moderator: 'If you do intend to withdraw, Mr Kane, then, you will understand, we would require an appropriate - and full - explanation.' The younger brother presented as calm, but Kane noted that he was now repeatedly rubbing and irritating the red, strawberry birthmark on his chin.

Kane stared at the floor for a time, then, when he looked up, he saw three pairs of eyes staring at him: the eyes of the two brothers and the incredulous solicitor. The Advocate made a faltering start: 'I…um…I worked it out. How you did it, I mean…'

The older brother guffawed: 'You make no sense, sir…'

'…I mean the hanging…how you staged the hanging…'

The younger brother shook his head and rubbed his reddening chin: "Staged?', Mr Kane, surely…'

'Cleverly done, I'm bound to say, with the other individuals involved entirely unaware of their own contribution…'

'Balderdash, sir.'

'But the plan had to work out just so, otherwise all was lost. The night before the hanging, you send a group of

Medical students to the well-known local hostelry where the hangman, George Gibney is wont to drink. And - having located him - they repeatedly send him over more and more rum. There was no earthly reason to do that - other than it was a part of a larger plan…'

Jack Balloch shook his head and sat back in his chair: 'Pshaw!' He turned to his younger brother: 'Do we have to keep listening to this bilge?'

Balloch the Younger placed his finger to his lips to quiet his older brother and motioned for the Advocate to go on. Kane continued: 'Whether it was the sheer quantity of alcohol, or whether those students had access to something to guarantee fogginess for the hangman the next day - the day of the hanging - is perhaps irrelevant - but suffice to say that on the day, George Gibney was well and truly off his game.'

A hush had descended on the room. Kane looked around the room. The faces of the brothers, smiling, seemed to be focused on the floor. Only the solicitor stared at Kane, face puzzled. The younger brother looked up: 'Ingenious, Mr Kane, but you forget - several thousand people witnessed the hanging itself…'

Kane cut in: 'They were fooled. They witnessed what looked like a hanging, but it was no more a genuine threat to life than…'. he was lost for words for a moment, but then remembered his conversation with Mr Horse, '…than a fairground conjuror sawing a lady in half.'

The older Balloch had had enough. He pushed back his chair, gave a grunt, got up and stood at the table. He picked up his deck of cards and began to deal them. The younger brother grinned and gave his chin a rub: 'Proceed, Mr Kane - this *is* fascinating.'

'Your brother there mounted the scaffold dressed as if for winter? Shivering with cold? Pretence. In fact, you had fashioned him a harness - much like the one you wear yourself under your shirt - that could be attached to the rope.'

The younger brother nodded. It was difficult to tell if he was agreeing or just considering what was being said. Kane continued: 'And when the time came, you asked for a private moment to say a prayer into your brother's ear - and while doing so, you attached the harness to the rope so that it could bear the weight…'

Alexander Balloch gave a little laugh: 'You are very clever, Mr Kane - but you are forgetting something…'

'Such as?'

'The rope, Mr Kane. The noose was placed around my brother's neck and the rope alone would have done the trick. So much for your ingenious theories. Now…'

But Kane held up a hand to interrupt him: 'No - the rope was ineffective for two reasons: One - your Medical students had ensured that it received a good soaking the night before, didn't they. That would have had an effect on its ability to tighten as a noose.'

Young Balloch smiled. 'And 'two'?'

'And two: your brother there wore a protective collar - probably made of wood - under his own raised collar…'

The younger Balloch laughed out loud now: 'Oh, Mr Kane - I do hope that your legal submissions today are not as fanciful as your theories. A wooden collar…'

Kane pressed on: 'You had such a collar made. A local haberdasher remembers being asked to make such an unusual item…'

'Nonsense…'

'…and the person who asked him to make such a thing, apparently, was of perfectly ordinary appearance…'

'Well, then..,'

'…apart from a curious birthmark in his chin. The haberdasher said that it was as if the chap's chin had been dipped in jam.'

At this point, the younger Balloch's chin looked as if it had been dipped in jam.

*****

Chapter Seventeen

Death. Again.

The discourse in the prison cell was suddenly interrupted by a loud laugh. It came from the older brother standing at the table. He was shaking his head at his younger brother: 'Oh, Sandy, Sandy, I'm afraid that our nefarious plan has been discovered. Allow me to complete the narrative before I die of boredom - again.' He did not look at Kane, but spoke almost absent-mindedly as he turned the cards: 'The physician on top of the cart, the one who signed the death certificate, let's just say that he was not exactly top of the class when he was my student. He did not, in fact, examine….what shall I call my deceased self…'the body'. He simply recorded what my brother was telling him about the vital signs – the breathing, the pulse and what-not.' He raised his head: 'Oh – look!' – and the older Balloch raised his arm for a moment, then let it drop down onto his side. 'No sign of life. Obviously dead.' Balloch laughed: 'And that was what was recorded on the Certificate. Ingenious - no?'

Kane was puzzled. Why was he admitting to this? Why now? The older brother was scowling now. He pointed at the spread of cards in the table. He shook his head: 'Death….again…'

Kane closed his eyes. The room had taken on a dream-like quality. He looked over at Phipps, his instructing solicitor, who was now sitting apparently frozen, his pen suspended in air, resembling a waxwork in Madame Tussaud's Baker Street Bazaar.

The younger Balloch was sitting, nodding and…what was that look on his face? Was he grinning? Smirking? The older Balloch stood at the table fussing over his cards. Kane had the sudden thought of being a helpless fly caught in the web of two malevolent spiders. The younger doctor broke the spell: 'I'm afraid, my brother, that we may well have been found out.' The older brother fussed over the cards: 'Death. Again.' He looked at Kane. 'The cards no doubt foretell the end…the end of my captivity here.' He frowned, then produced his watch from his pocket and studied it: 'Look at the time, gentlemen. Time, I think, to summon the warder. I assume that my transport to the court has been arranged?'

The solicitor, Mr Phipps, had been silent during the entirely of the revelations, but shook himself out of it and felt compelled to speak now. He looked across to Alexander Balloch: 'But…but…Dr Balloch…you have both just confessed that the whole thing…the whole thing…was…'

The younger Balloch smirked and shook his head: 'My dear, Mr Phipps, I have done no such thing. Everything that the Advocate, Mr Kane has suggested today may well be quite true. That is conceded.' He nodded towards Kane: 'My congratulations, sir, on assembling a difficult puzzle. But,' he held up his finger to accentuate his point, 'but what you heard was not a *confession*.' He grinned. 'Was it, Mr Kane?'

The young Advocate narrowed his eyes for a moment. And then, with a realisation, nodded and gave a small sigh. Balloch pointed to Kane and then to the solicitor: 'I shall let the Advocate earn his corn.'

Kane looked over at the solicitor: 'It was not a confession, Mr Phipps. It was part of a consultation…'

The younger Balloch grinned: 'Meaning?'

'…meaning that both you and I, Mr Phipps, are bound by our oaths of confidentiality in respect of what we have just heard.'

A broad smile on Balloch's face: 'And who, pray, are you allowed to tell about anything that you have just heard?'

Kane said nothing for a moment, then: 'No-one. We can tell no-one at all.'

The older brother, Jack Balloch, called over: 'And did I forget to mention that I knew what I was doing when I gave our old father that fatal dose? Doddery old fool. At the end, he was good to neither man nor beast. But no need to tell anyone that.' He laughed: 'I've already been found guilty of killing him. What more can they do to me?'

The younger brother, Alexander Balloch got up from his chair and stretched his problematic back: 'Shall we get our coats? Mustn't keep those judges waiting…'

*****

Just as Edward Kane thought that the situation could not become any more surreal, he found himself standing waiting in the muddy, crowded courtyard of Calton Jail compelled to make polite conservation with a man who had just admitted to poisoning his father, had been hanged 'until dead', had been apparently revived and who was now about to be the subject of a court hearing, the likes of which had not been heard in over a hundred years.

They stood there and waited for the cart that would ferry Dr Jack Balloch to court – and freedom? The prisoner was in good spirits: 'I meant to say that you seemed awfully vexed the other day, Mr Kane, when I read your cards…' The young Advocate - keen not to engage - tried to keep it short: 'I do not care for divination, Dr Balloch.' The doctor continued - whether Kane wanted to hear it or not: 'It was the 'Death' card, wasn't it, Mr Kane? To the un-initiated, I can understand why that might appear problematic and perhaps somewhat frightening. However,' and here he gave a broad smile, 'the Death card has many meanings. Not least, the prospect of 'release'. Release from worries, or from financial woes, or from a difficult situation. In the Death card, Mr Kane, you should understand that it is the *problem* that 'dies' - not the person.' He gave a little chuckle. 'I have been drawing the card all day. No doubt, because we are about to see my release - on account of your excellent legal submissions, sir.'

This last comment made Kane squirm (not a little). He had yet to formulate the acceptable reason for his possible withdrawal from acting to be put before the collection of testy judges ahead.

This stilted conversation was interrupted by the arrival of the horse and cart. The conveyance to court comprised a driver in the box and two police escorts inside, both stovepipe-hatted in blue jackets with brass buttons.

The driver jumped down: 'Apologies, gentlemen. We're going slow today.' He gave the horse's neck an affectionate slap: 'When Maggie here has one of her crabbit days, then - watch out.' On hearing this, Balloch nudged Kane and hissed: 'You hear that, Kane - it is a sign! They have brought a 'Maggie' to secure my freedom.' He winked:

'Although, this Maggie does not look 'Half-Hangit'.' He guffawed. Balloch turned to the warder behind him and held up his hands: 'I wonder, good sir, if you could remove these manacles? I rather think that the two police officers inside the cart will be sufficient to secure my safe delivery to the courts. And I can assure you - I have no desire to escape. I know that my release is imminent now.' The warder gave an inquiring look to the police officers on the cart. They looked back and gave a couple of indifferent nods. Their daily stock-in-trade would involve violent criminals, so a genteel middle-aged doctor was unlikely to tax them overly.

The shackles were removed. Sandy Balloch, the younger brother, smiled and handed the prisoner his hat and walking cane. The convict, Jack Balloch put on his hat, leered over at Kane and the solicitor: 'Ahhhh. That's better. You see, gentlemen - Death in the cards begins with a release from chains. Now…' He walked over and began to scrutinise the near-decrepit horse that was to pull him to court. 'So, this is the engine of my freedom, is it?' He frowned: 'How old is this animal?' The driver shrugged: 'No-one knows, sir. She was a barge horse for some years before she came into the service.'

Balloch walked to the front of the horse and pulled open its lips with a rough tug: 'Look at all those missing teeth. This nag is older than the hills. I'm surprised that they didn't feed it to Napoleon's soldiers at Waterloo.' He walked backwards, laughing, amused at his own joke. 'Still - we'll get her moving and get me to the court on time - even if we require to…' Balloch thwacked his walking cane onto the palm of his hand.

And that's when it happened.

Maggie - the horse in question - was so alarmed by the apparent threat of the cane that she kicked up her hind legs.

Afterwards, witnesses described it as if the animal had been struck by lightning, making her back legs shoot out. The result was a hoof striking Dr Jack Balloch in the face. He, in turn, was thrown backwards (both cane and hat flying in the air) landing in an undignified heap in the mud. Fortunately, another doctor was present - younger brother, Sandy Balloch: 'Jack! Jack! Are you alright?' Jack?'

*****

Mr Horse stroked his stubbly chin: 'Dead, Mr K? Dead?'

Edward Kane, Advocate, sat back in his wing chair by the fire, nursing a glass of rum and milk in his hand: 'Dead as a dodo, Mr Horse. The kick of that old horse broke Balloch's neck.'

Horse whistled: 'Would you Adam and Eve it, sir! The bloke survives the hangman's drop - but then gets his neck broke by a horse.' He grinned. 'Wait a minute, wait a minute - knowing them brothers – are you sure it weren't just a pantomime horse that they hired for the day?'

Kane laughed: 'The only theatricality appeared to be the response of the younger brother. In floods of tears. Except, on this occasion - as opposed to last time - the tears were real.'

Horse took a puff of his long clay pipe and shook his head: 'Would you credit it, sir. And what did the judges have to say when you got to court?'

Kane nodded: 'They seemed relieved.'

'And what were they gonna do, sir? The judges, I mean, if your man Dr Balloch hadn't snuffed it.'

Kane sat forward in his chair: 'Oddly enough, I encountered Lord Eriskay in Parliament Hall afterwards and he thanked me for all my hard work. I broached with him the subject of a possible answer and…'

'And?'

'…and Lord Eriskay laughed, took a coin out of his pocket and tossed it in the air.'

Horse laughed: 'Haha - heads or tails! Maybe you should have given the judges a deck of them Tarot cards, sir. That might have helped with an answer.'

The Advocate raised his index finger. 'On that subject, Horse…' Kane got up from his chair and went over to his work bag. '…as we were parting, the younger Balloch brother insisted that I have these.' He produced the deck of Tarot cards that had so obsessed the now twice-departed Dr Jack Balloch. 'He said he couldn't bear to look at them any more.' He handed the cards to his manservant.

Horse studied the faces of the cards: 'Never understood these, sir.' He pursed his lips: 'Did I ever tell you that my old nan had 'The Sight'?'

Kane gave a good-humoured groan: 'Not *recently*, Mr Horse.'

'A wery wise woman, my old nan. Used to read the tea leaves, she did.'

'And what did she predict for you, my friend?'

'Funny enough - she said I would have a lot of dealings with The Law…'

They both laughed.

Mr Horse studied the cards again. 'My nan said that sometimes the bad luck sticks to the thing and not the person. That doctor - he was looking for these cards to bring him luck. I wonder if he was looking at them when he decided to do away with his poor old dad.'

'We will never know, Mr Horse.'

Horse sighed: 'Maybe it's the cards themselves that's cursed, sir. I think we should get rid of them'

Kane (a good Son of the Manse) nodded: 'Amen to that, Mr Horse. I'm happy that you dispose of them how you will. They could be sold, perhaps?'

Horse shook his head: 'The fella what loved these cards loved them more than his own father, Mr K. Only one thing for them.' Horse got up from his stool and walked to the fireplace. There he stood before the blazing fire and, one by one, he drew each card from the deck, looked at the card for a moment, then tossed each single card into the flames, naming it as it went:

'And there goes The Juggler…'

Toss.

'And here's a bloke holding up what looks like a sword and some scales. Don't know what that is…'

Kane volunteered: "Justice', perhaps?'

'Justice! Into the fire with it…'

Toss.

'And here's Old Nick. The Devil, himself.' He wagged his finger at the card and spoke to it: 'In you get, Nick! You'll be used to all them flames, my son…'

Toss.

'And…wait a minute…what's this. Oh, no…' Horse suddenly appeared worried.

Kane leaned forward in his chair: 'Horse - what is it?'

'This card sir - I think I recognise it…'

'What is it?'

Horse shook his head: 'Trouble, sir. Serious trouble coming to our door. A horrible thing…and it wants…it wants…'

Kane was worried now: 'What does it want, Horse?'

The manservant's face broke into a grin: 'Sorry, sir. For a minute there, I thought it was a picture of the landlady - looking for last month's rent…'

Kane shook his head: 'Mr Horse, I fear that you have missed your vocation.'

'As a fortune-teller, sir?'

'As an actor on the comic stage. Now, can I invite you to turn away from such things and towards our supper? A supper, devoid this time, I hope, of any trace of canine scraps…'

'If you give me a minute, sir.'

Horse continued to study each card, then toss it into the fire.

Kane smiled and shook his head: 'Mr Horse….'

'Nearly there, sir - is that a castle struck by lightning?'

'Supper, Mr Horse?'

'Blimey - here's a woman - looks like she's dressed up like The Pope, sir…'

Kane laughed: 'Mr Horse – if you please - supper!!!'

'Bloomin' heck, Mr K – wait 'til you see this next one…'

*****

BONUS STORY

Aunty Fran and 'Tickler'

Funny, isn't it, how at this time of year, your thoughts turn to the people that you've lost.

Whenever I open my Christmas presents, I always think of Aunty Fran.

She was unstoppable, my Aunty Fran. Just a real life force. You know how, when some people come into a room and the whole place just lights up? Well, Aunty Fran was one of those people.

Born in Edinburgh in 1928. Can you imagine it? 1928! She used to say 'The only thing older than me is Jenners...'.

And how she used to rail about the modern generation! 'If you wrap yourself in cotton wool then how are you supposed to feel anything?' she used to say.

But Christmas and New Year were her best times. You never knew what Aunty Fran would give you. Some years, it would be a big box of sweeties or similar, and the next year something bizarre.

One year I opened the wrapping and there was another parcel inside. And then another parcel inside that. And then, like a set of Russian dolls, I had to open seven parcels to get to the contents. And when I did, all that the parcel contained was a small, white stone. I was ten at the time. I wasn't well pleased. I looked up at my aunty, but Fran was beaming: 'Look at this stone! I picked it specially for you, dear. At Portobello beach.' She nodded towards it: 'Read it.' And when I looked at it carefully, she had written in tiny wee writing: 'And when I am gone/This stone will be here/Remember I love you/A million, my dear.' I had to laugh. The other gifts are long gone now, but I still have the stone.

And then, of course, there was 'Tickler'. Tickler was the pet name for Aunty Fran's violin. I always assumed that she had given it that name because whenever she played it, people would start to smile and laugh.

Oh, Christmas Day was a treat. She used to come to our house with Tickler. She had a battered old book of Christmas Carols and she would shepherd us all around it and we would sing 'O Little Town of Bethlehem' and 'Silent Night' and what have you, and she would play the tune on the violin. She made fun of the whole thing at one level, but that violin always sounded so sweet to me.

Then - at New Year - she was...what did I call her, again...'unstoppable'. Tickler would be produced from its battered old case and the room would be jumping with jigs and reels and we would fling our heads back and throw each other about. Then she would slow the music right down and play those great Burns songs, 'My Love is Like a Red, Red, Rose.' or 'Ae Fond Kiss' and - to my ears - the violin itself would sound as if it was crying with longing and regret.

She never married. Of course, being Fran, she had many proposals of marriage (even into her seventies) but she turned them all down.

I remember once at New Year, after we had seen in The Bells, and when everybody else had gone to bed, Aunty Fran and I were the last ones still up. It must have been three o'clock in the morning. And the whisky and the exhaustion were setting in and I asked her if she had ever been in love. She nodded and said: 'Once...but it was impossible.'

Near the end of the War - this would have been some time late in 1944 - her father had been stationed back in Edinburgh.

Fran said that she and her school friends used to help with the war effort – collecting old bits of scrap metal or knitting socks and scarves for 'our boys overseas'.

Now back in Edinburgh, Fran's father was stationed at Donaldson's School near Haymarket. I thought it was only a school for the deaf, but Fran said that during the War, it was used as a Prisoner of War camp for Italian and German soldiers who had been captured. All the schoolchildren had been moved out to North Berwick and the like in case of air raids. Can you imagine that? Donaldson's School in Edinburgh - a Prisoner of War camp?

Fran said that she and her school friend, Wee Ina, used to walk past Donaldson's on their way to school and peer through the gates at the prisoners. And, of course - Fran being Fran - she started to wave at some of them as she passed. And one or two of them started to wave back. She laughed: 'Can you imagine? I was fifteen or sixteen, walking along a street in Edinburgh - and waving at the Nazis!'

Before long, Fran and Ina would talk to some of the younger prisoners through the bars. 'And their English - it was perfect. It was much better than Ina's. But then, Ina's from Paisley...'

Christmas was coming. This would have been late 1944. There was one of the young prisoners that Fran particularly liked. 'Kurt' was his name. He was about 17. A good-looking boy. Curly blond hair. German. And every morning, as Fran and Ina made their way to school, Kurt would be lingering about the fence for a chat. And then again on the way home.

It wasn't long before Fran started to feel sorry for the young soldier cooped up in the west wing of that great building. She asked about his family. No family. She asked about his friends. No friends. It soon became obvious that he was just a boy caught up in the whole tide of war - and captured straight away. Brought up just outside a tiny German village, Kurt said that he had only ended up joining the army because he had been conscripted. He hated the whole thing.

And then, it happened that during one of their chats, Fran mentioned that she and Ina were going to the cinema on Christmas Eve. She was astonished to learn that Kurt - who had been brought up on a farm - had never seen a film. Never. And so, the plan was hatched. She recalled:

'You see, Ina had a big brother and he had just left school, and they still had his school uniform in the house. We told Kurt that we would smuggle him out of Donaldson's on Christmas Eve, get the school uniform on him and then take him to the flicks.'

'Weren't you afraid he'd escape?'

'Och, no. He was just a wee lad, really. And where was he gonnae go? Glasgow?? Wi' a German accent? He would have opened his mouth and they would have stuck the head on him...'

Fran knew the changeover schedule from her father's own shifts at Donaldson's and she and Ina knew many of the soldiers on guard already, and so the escape went flawlessly at a vulnerable point in the fence - as Ina flirted shamelessly with one of the guards.

Fran laughed: 'Oh, you should have seen Kurt's face when we got him out. He changed into the clothes we brought and we walked along Gorgie Road. He couldn't believe how beautiful Edinburgh was. You would have thought that Gorgie was Paradise..

'So, we took him up to the Pooles Roxy Cinema on Gorgie Road - one of the big picture houses at the time - I think it's all been made into flats now. It was just getting dark when we got there - and the crowds! You should have seen it. It was worse than Tynecastle on a Saturday. I'm not exaggerating - there must have been over a thousand people there on Christmas Eve queuing the see that film. I mean, what else was there to do in those days? And there were police everywhere. And Ina and I are standing there with an escaped prisoner of war...'. And at that point, Fran burst into fits of laugher.

'So what did you do?'

'Well, I had an aunty who worked there as the projectionist - the fella who was normally there was away fighting in France - so I got one of the ushers to go and get her. And she came out and took us inside - you should have seen the looks on people's faces as we skipped the queue - and then she sort of planked us at the back of the cinema.'

'What film was it?"

Fran thought for a moment, then: 'Well, there was a cartoon, then a newsreel and then one of thone Bing Crosby films where he was playing a priest...which one? 'Bells of St Mary's'...no, it was 'Going My Way'! He was aye playing a priest in those days - when he wasn't singing the 'White Christmas''

Fran smiled: 'And you should have seen the look on wee Kurt's face when that picture started. As I said, he'd never been to the pictures before and he was bamboozled by the whole thing.'

We sat in silence while Fran sipped at her whisky. Her mood changed as the memories overcame her: 'And there was this bit in the film where Bing - or should I say 'Father Bing' - was singing with a lot of wee laddies, you know, a boys' choir thing, and they all started singing 'Silent Night' in their wee high voices, and my pal Ina nudged me in the ribs, and I looked over at Kurt - and he was crying. Just tears running down that boy's face. And I don't know why, but I started crying as well. And then Ina starting crying an' all, and the three of us were in a right state.

'Anyway, after the picture, we got him back to Donaldson's and Ina did that thing with the guard again, so we snuck Kurt back through the fence. But before he went in, he looked into my eyes and he held me by the shoulders. And he leaned down, and he kissed me on the lips. And I just stood there. It was all very innocent.' Fran ran her finger across her lips at this point, re-tracing the memory. 'I remember it was so soft and gentle. It was like...'. she laughed to herself '...like a wee child kissing you goodnight.'

Fran finished her drink. 'So the next day was Christmas. My dad was on an early shift at Donaldson's, and when he came home that day he was carrying a violin case. He said to me: 'Yer wee pal, the curly heided Jerry boy, the nice lad, said that this was a present for you.' I opened the case and inside was this battered old violin and a note 'To the lovely

Fran. For your great kindness. It was like a beautiful dream. One day when it is all over, I hope that we can bing together again. Fröhliche Weihnachten. With deepest affection. Kurt.'

'I couldn't speak or read any German, so I handed my dad the note. He read it: 'It means 'Merry Christmas'.' Then he laughed. 'A nice boy - but his spelling isn't up to much, is it? 'bing again', when it should be 'sing again...'. I smiled to myself and said nothing. Dad pointed to the violin: 'Oh, and he said that he had a name for the violin - 'The Tickler'. 'The Tickler'!' My dad laughed: 'And they say that these German boys have no sense of humour..."

*****

On their first day back at school, Fran and Ina waited at the gates of Donaldson's - but no sign of Kurt. When her dad got home, he explained that some of the German prisoners had been moved to another camp. 'Camp 21', somewhere out in Perthshire. Kurt had been one of them. In those days, during the war, everything was hush-hush, so it was impossible to find out anything more. Many years later, when Fran tried to track down what happened to Kurt, she was told that the relevant prisoner records had been destroyed - when a German bomb had hit the official building.

*****

Near the end, when Fran was in hospital (when the doctor told her of her condition, she said 'Well - I suppose you've got to die of something...') and when I was visiting, she said that she had a present for me. She pointed to one of those wee bedside lockers, reached under her pillow and took out a key. I opened the locker, and there, in its battered old case, was Tickler.

'Now, dear, if you look in the case, you'll find an address and a phone number of one of the posh auction houses. Promise me you'll take it there. It'll be worth something,' and at that point she gave me a cheeky wink ' - but never, NEVER take the first offer!'

True to my promise, about a week later, I attended at the auction house. I was taken into a back room and was introduced to one of the valuers. I explained the circumstances, and he laughed. I handed over the battered violin case. And when he opened it, he smiled and he shook his head, and I'm sure that I heard him mutter: 'Oh, Tickler...'

I looked up: 'You've seen it before?'

He nodded: 'Oh, yes. Some years ago, when your aunt was in financial straits. But she was reluctant to part with it....'

I nodded. 'I suppose it's a sort of family heirloom. She's asked me to offer it for sale. Would you like to buy it?'

He looked down at the battered old instrument and frowned. I pressed on: 'I would be willing to take a fair price...'

The valuer sighed: 'Your aunt refused two hundred...'

Now, what was it that Fran had stressed? NEVER take the first offer! 'Well,' I stammered, 'two hundred pounds is not really a lot of money these days...'

The valuer looked at me as if I was stupid: 'Two hundred pounds??? It was two hundred thousand...she was offered two hundred thousand pounds...'. He looked at the violin again and sighed: 'We could perhaps go to two hundred and fifty...after all, it is a Tecchler...'

Turns out that the pet name for the violin had been taken from its real name - 'Tecchler'. One of those rare, old violins a bit like a Stradivarius. Apparently, this one had been made in the 1700s.

But Fran hadn't known that at the time. On that dream-like night in 1944, as the bombs were falling over Europe, she had shown another young person nothing but kindness, expecting no reward, and the young German soldier had given Fran the most precious thing that he had - and she had kept it close to her, as one would keep a precious memory.

*****

Fran died last year at the age of 91. Untypically quiet, she left us peacefully - but with a smile on her face - and with her family around her bed.

Tickler is gone too. A fair price was agreed and it paid off my parents' mortgage and gave me a nice deposit for my wee flat. Isn't Edinburgh property dear!

Funny how at this time of year, your thoughts turn to those no longer with us.

I can't pass Donaldson's school without thinking of Aunty Fran. It's all luxury flats now, but sometimes, when I'm passing, maybe on the top deck of a bus, I look down, and in my mind's eye, I see that wartime schoolgirl running across those grounds, laughing with her young German prisoner in tow.

I'll always think of Aunty Fran whenever I'm unwrapping my Christmas presents (however many layers).

And I still have that wee stone…

*****

Thanks to…

Sir Sandy McCall Smith for his constant encouragement and support.

Colin, Douglas, Mike and Gordon – when shall we five meet again?

Alistair Johnson – Incomparable Faculty Librarian!

Alan Young, Editor of The Scotsman.

Iain Livingstone @ Scottish Print – scottishprint.com – for his keen eye and printing prowess.

Chris Mackinnon – Man of Many Talents.

Andy, Walker and '*The Friends of Mr B*'.

And, of course, Lesley-Anne. My soulmate.

Only forever.

If you have enjoyed this book, then don't miss the other books in the series:

Edward Kane and Mr Horse – Collected Short Stories: Vol I

And the full-length novel

Edward Kane and the Parlour Maid Murderer

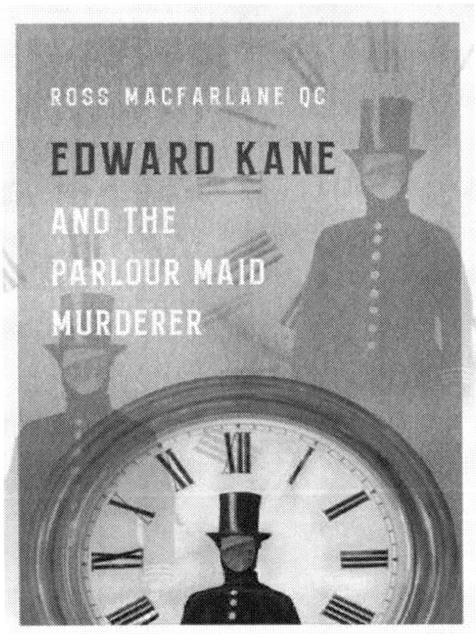

Available now from Amazon and Kindle.

Printed in Dunstable, United Kingdom

74837279R00167